D0889312

Fireflies

by Mary Peace

For Elizabeth,

I hope you enjoy reading Mark's story.

Mary Peace

Published by
COPPLE HOUSE BOOKS, INC.
Lakemont, Georgia 30552

Library of Congress Cataloging-in-Publication Data

Peace Mary, 1942 —
  Fireflies.
    I. Title.
  PZ7.P3Fi 1986   [Fic]   86-4540
  ISBN 0-932298-45-1

            Summary
  His rapidly expanding extrasensory abilities lead high
  school senior, Mark Miller, into strange and often unwanted
  "knowings" and cause increasing difficulties in his relation-
  ships with other people, especially with his girlfriend, Becky.

  [1. Extrasensory perception — Fiction. 2. Self-acceptance
  Fiction. 3. High schools — Fiction. 4. Schools — Fiction]

Manufactured in the United States of America

to

Ruth and Joe

Chapter One

It was Friday, last period — 2:10 P.M. — Senior English. The drone of Mrs. Bethune's nasal twang buzzed, irritating Mark's ears, like a fly he couldn't brush away. He leaned back in his seat, tuning in only enough to answer a question, pass a test, and let his eyes roam across his classmates' backs. Who would it be this time?

Because she responded so quickly, because he had a hard time not watching her, he chose Becky. He focused slightly below the clasp on the gold chain he had given her, just under her wavy black hair. Then, relaxing his concentration, following the pattern he'd established, he pressed the stem on his digital stop watch. Not thinking anything in particular, he kept his eyes fixed on that spot on Becky's pink sweater. Seconds passed, then, predictably, she squirmed, shifted in her chair, and finally, turned to glance back over her shoulder.

Mark lowered his eyes, purposely not making contact, and checked the time. Forty-five seconds. He grinned.

He surveyed the room again, zeroing in this time on Harley. Good old Harley. His antidote to boredom was too blatant to fool even Mrs. Bethune. His right hand rose and fell to the rhythmic invention playing in his head. He was probably another Beethoven — child prodigy, musical genius, flake. His head was so full of music he could hardly cross the street without getting run over, but he was a good guy, and a challenge.

Mark's look bored into Harley's neck, then he made himself relax. *It doesn't work to try so hard.* He pushed the stem on the stop watch and waited. Harley's foot joined in the beat as his right hand grabbed at a pencil and scribbled something on the manuscript paper tucked inside his English book. Mark pushed his thoughts aside, kept himself from checking the watch, stared.

" — and the signficance of the symbolism in the passage that follows where — " Mrs. Bethune's analysis grated on and on.

Finally Harley jerked back, rubbed his neck, hunched his shoulders and lost the beat. His body, seemingly confused by the discovery that it was sitting in Senior English, squared itself, and suddenly his head whipped around, almost catching Mark off guard.

Two minutes, fifty-one seconds. A long time. Mark grinned again. But Harley *had* turned. *Wonder why it's so different with Harley?* And then he wondered why he even cared. He'd started doing this dumb experiment, partly by accident, partly to keep from going to sleep in Mrs. Bethune's class. His "A" could plummet quickly if she caught his eyes closed. Closed minds were out of her range, but closed eyes infuriated her.

"Mark." Mrs. Bethune's voice drew him to full attention. "Could you tell us the signficance of the symbol of water in these works?"

Mark's head raced as he drawled, "Y-yes," and then pulled out the perfect answer from his so-far reliable mental inventory. "It symbolizes life — the underlying, sustaining presence of life, and the assurance of renewal and hope."

"Thank you, Mark," Mrs. Bethune gushed.

Mark cringed but breathed a sigh of relief as the intercom from the school office crackled on. *May I have your attention, please.* It was the voice of Mr. Jaramillo, the school principal. *It's spring. The days are getting longer. Flowers are blooming. Bees are buzzing. You are falling in love.* A giggle of response went through the class. Becky glanced at Mark. *But* — Now his voice boomed with authority. *There will no longer be an official or unofficial school sanction of woodsies. Drinking on or off campus will result in expulsion and possible arrest.*

Mark could hear Mr. Jaramillo's breath quiver as he sighed over the speaker. *The school is adopting this hard-nosed policy — for your sake. We don't want an empty place at graduation again this year. That's all. Thank you.*

The class was somber, remembering last spring — the mangled car at the bottom of the ravine, empty beer cans still in a row along the dash board, and the coffin closing over the blue and gold of Pixie's cheerleader's outfit. But from his vantage point, Mark saw the indolent smirks that passed among Clay and Jake and Bunnie — Buxom Bunnie as everyone called her. So, they were planning another one. Well, *he* wouldn't be there, or any of his friends.

"Well, now, class as I was saying — " Mrs. Bethune seemed determined to use those last five minutes. The class groaned.

Mark leaned back and sighed. Thank goodness not every class was this deadly. He slipped into his private game, but without much interest. His eyes roamed over the class and came back to the three "toughs." That was one thing about Rolling Oaks High — labels. Everybody had one. Jocks were jocks. Freaks were freaks. Cowboys were cowboys. Straights were straights. Once you were labeled something, that's what you were, no matter what. Jake and Clay and Bunnie and their crowd were the worst — rowdies into drugs and sex and liquor and being mean.

He let himself target in on the straw blond of Bunnie's long, tough-sexy hair and linger there; then he pushed the stem of the stop watch. His mind went blank. As he waited, Jake's grungy tobacco and grease-stained hand slipped into his line of vision, its fingers intertwining in the straw blond strands. He saw Bunnie tense, then shudder. And suddenly Mark shuddered, too, and sat bolt upright, overcome with a sensation unlike anything he'd ever experienced. He felt — he felt it! He felt what Bunnie was feeling. It was as if those hands were in *his* hair. No longer watching Bunnie from outside, he was feeling her feelings inside, sensing the terrible savage fear gripping her.

Lights sparkled before his eyes. Then, as clearly as words spoken aloud, he *heard*. Bunnie's thoughts screamed in his head, *I can't stand this any more!*

The bell jangled. The link broke. Mark sat, stunned, staring after Bunnie, Jake's grasp on her hair propelling her in front of him out into the hall.

Chapter Two

Mark looked up into the puzzled expression on Becky's face. "Oh!" he exclaimed, jumping to his feet. "Let's get going."

"Why were you sitting there like that?" Becky asked.

"Just thinking, I guess." Then, shaking off the weird feeling, he joked, "I was overwhelmed by the significance of the symbol of water as it applies to —"

"Oh, you!" Becky swatted him with her notebook. "Come on. I've got to get at those ivories."

"And I've got to get to the drug store," Mark said, pushing the door open for her. "How are you doing, anyway?"

"Awful! I'm a bundle of nerves. Whenever I even think about tomorrow, my hands start to shake."

"You'll do fine," Mark said, hoping he was right. The last time he heard her piece, it was still pretty rocky in places. Try as hard as she might, Becky wasn't the natural musical genius Harley was. Hers came from work — lots of hard work. "Look, Beck, go home and practice until dinnertime, then forget about it. Harley and Francine and I will come by for you about 6:30. The game starts at 7:00."

"Well, I don't know —" She hesitated. "I should practice all evening —"

"Becky! That's silly. You can practice too much, you know."

"And besides —" Becky pouted. " — it won't be much fun watching the game without watching you play."

"Well," he growled, "if you're smart, you'll still be watching me." He lunged at her, eyes crossed, tongue hanging out.

"Oh, Mark —" She pushed him away. "Quit it!"

Mark glanced up just in time to flag down his bus. "Got to go, Beck. See you at 6:30." He dropped the coins in the box and found a window seat.

So, he thought, examining the feelings that had nearly bubbled to the surface with Becky's comment, I thought I was okay about not playing anymore. He did miss it, but when he'd decided to take the job at his dad's drug store, baseball had to go, even if he had been one of the best players. Having some spending money and saving for college next year were, after all, more important. Still —

Mark looked down out of the bus window, idly focusing on the driver's position in the car in the next lane. The driver, a lady, drove with her hands resting on the lower part of the steering wheel. Suddenly, the hands flexed around the wheel and she looked directly up at him, an astonished expression on her face.

Embarrassed, Mark smiled and nodded hello, then glanced away. The car sped ahead and out of sight.

What is going on with me? The experiment in class. Bunnie. Those spots in front of my eyes again. Now this. Curiosity whetted, he picked a second car. This time he watched from the corner of his eye, keeping his head straight. Another surprised driver turned and looked his way. Weird, Mark said to himself. Definitely weird.

He pushed away his crazy thoughts as he opened the drug store door and wove through the display cases to the back of the pharmacy. "Hi," he said, plopping his back pack down. "How's it going?"

"Forty, forty-five, fifty." His father finished counting aloud, scraping capsules through a little funnel and into a prescription bottle. "Oh, not too bad," he said, looking up. "It's been a slow day. How was school?"

"Slow there, too. I'm glad it's Friday. I still get the day off tomorrow, don't I?"

"Oh, yes," his dad chuckled. "I guess I don't expect to see too much of you down here until after graduation. And besides, I certainly wouldn't want to answer to Becky if I made you come in tomorrow. How's she doing?"

"Scared. We're going to the game tonight."

His dad gave him a knowing look, but if he was tempted, he didn't say anything more than, "Good. Maybe we can leave a little early."

"Okay by me," Mark agreed.

"How did you know I was watching you?" Mark said before he realized that the question was a confession. He'd been practicing his "evil eye" since they left the store.

"I felt it," his dad said. "Why *were* you looking at me like that?"

Mark didn't want to admit the real reason. "Because you're so handsome?" he joked.

"No, you may not have the car tonight," his dad laughed, "if that's what you're buttering me up for. Oh, by the way," he added, "speaking of cars, your mom's going to drive me to my conference tomorrow so she can have my car and you can take the other one to Music Contest." His car was the new sleek silver Mercury Marquis with the conservative metallic door sign, "Miller's Rexall Drug. We serve your Rx needs. 924-3000." That car — the image — was supposed to be good for business, but Mark almost never got to drive it. The one he drove was the old family car, an unpretentious Ford Fairlane that was sitting in the driveway as they pulled in.

Mark followed his dad in through the front door and groaned as the delicious aroma of roasting chicken knotted his stomach. "Oh, Mom!" he yelled, "it smells great! I'm starved. When do we eat?"

"Hi, you two," Mom greeted them giving his dad a hug. "You're early. It'll be a few minutes."

"Ohhh!" Mark sank onto a kitchen chair, feigning weakness, then slid onto the floor under the table. "Oh!" he said, surprised. "Hello, Napoleon." Napoleon indignantly turned his superior green eyes on Mark as if to say, "You've invaded my territory."

"Cats!" Mark muttered. "Nappy, I'd turn you into a dog if I could."

He glared back at Napoleon, trying out his "evil eye." Napoleon grumbled. Then he pulled his paws up under him. Muscles rippled under the fur on his back.

Napoleon stared. Mark stared back. Deadlock. Then suddenly, ears flattened to his head, Napoleon took off running at full speed and disappeared.

"Ha!" Mark hooted.

"What did you do to my cat?" Mom's voice accused.

"Nothing, Mom. Just looking." He laughed. "Crazy cat."

By game time, Mark no longer regretted that he wouldn't be playing. It would be nice to sit with Becky. The doorbell rang, and he could hear Francine's giggle outside. "Hi," he said, "come on in."

"Hello, Francine. Hello, Harley," his mom called from the kitchen. "Are you ready for Music Contest tomorrow?"

"Oh, sure." Harley shrugged. "Ready as I'll ever be."

"You're playing your own composition this year."

Harley nodded, as usual, unimpressed.

"Well, good luck!"

"Bye, Mom," Mark said, then spotting Napoleon added, "Bye, dumb cat. Hey —" He stopped. "Want to see something funny?"

"Sure," Francine agreed. "What?"

"Hey, Nappy," he whispered at the cat. Napoleon looked up and Mark gave him a killer-cat look that sent Napoleon fleeing helter-skelter back through the kitchen.

Francine and Harley burst into laughter.

"Za power of za evil eye." Mark tried to sound wicked.

The living room window at Becky's house was open, and Mendelssohn escaped outside and flowed down the street to meet them.

"Well, she's still at it," Francine said.

"Yep," Harley agreed. His hand, uncontrollably caught up in the music, began to conduct. At first, Mark didn't know why Harley groaned, but the next boo-boo was evident even to him. Then crash! The dissonance that followed could only have been Becky's hands slamming down on the piano keys.

"Oh, no," Francine moaned, hanging back. "You'd better go in first, Mark. We'll wait here."

"No." Mark shook his head. "No way. Harley, maybe you can do something. Beck?" he called, then rang the doorbell.

The door opened to a red-faced Becky. "Oh, I can't go!" she wailed. "I just can't get this stupid passage. I'm going to practice it until I do it right, even if it takes all night."

The three watched her, not speaking, knowing it was no use to argue. Finally Mark said, "Uh, may we come in?"

Becky shrugged. "If you want to," she said, and flounced back over to the piano, glaring daggers. Hands poised, she slammed into the passage once more, like a hit-and-run driver, massacring victims along the way. Harley edged slowly up to the piano and slid onto the end of the bench. "Uh, Becky," he said softly, "maybe you could try this." He played the arpeggio — without even seeing the music, Mark noticed — in a dah-da-da, dah-da-da, long-short-short, long-short-short rhythm.

"That makes it even harder," Becky wailed.

"Try it," Harley urged.

A few minutes later, Becky sailed through the troublesome arpeggio without a flaw. "Oh, Harley!" she said, throwing her arms around his neck, "you're terrific. Thanks!"

"Well!" Mark said, feigning jealousy. "I'd have helped if I could have." He went to the piano and picked Becky's hands up off the keys. "Now can we go to the game? We're already late."

Cries from a few enthusiastic fans echoed in the chilly spring night, drawing the foursome quickly through the gate and up into the bleachers. Rolling Oaks High was behind, Mark noted with disappointment. If only — he stopped himself from thinking it. He wasn't and that was that.

One of Mark's teammates — *ex*teammates, Tom, was stepping up to bat. "Knock it out of the field, Tom," Mark yelled. Becky and Francine joined in. At least they could drum up some spirit, he thought. Attendance at baseball games was nothing like it was for football, and he knew it helped to have someone pulling for you on the sidelines.

Tom swung at the ball and missed.

"Come on, Tom!" Mark hollered, then shifting his attention to the opposing team's pitcher, he watched his showy wind-up. *If I can turn people around with a single look, maybe there's more I can do — Maybe I can still help my team.* He narrowed his eyes, penetrating the pitcher with his stare. *You're going to throw wild.*

"Hit it, Tom!" Becky yelled at his side.

Wild pitch. Wild. Mark concentrated. Just as the ball shot from the pitcher's hand, a searing pain ripped through Mark's forehead, a pain so intense that it forced his eyes closed. Only the sharp crack of bat against ball and Becky pounding on his shoulder and screaming, "Go, go, go!" let him know the pitch hadn't been wild.

"Homerun!" Becky yelled, turning to Mark. "Did you see that? What's the matter?" Her excitement was swallowed up in concern.

"I-I have a headache," Mark said, slowly opening his eyes. "It's getting better. Look, I think I'll go get us some Cokes." He stood. The pain was subsiding, but he felt he needed to do something. "I'll be right back." He edged in front of the others and stepped carefully down the bleachers. The concession stand wasn't busy and he bought the four Cokes and sipped his. Had he done that to himself? Somehow brought on that pain? What *was* going on in his head, anyhow?

Mark was just starting back when he saw a shadowy movement under the bleachers. He stepped out of the bright light to see better.

A group of six or seven kids were huddled around a

bottle-shaped paper sack, passing it around. A big lot of good Mr. Jaramillo's talk did, Mark thought. He started on but suddenly, from within that group, long strawberry blond strands caught his attention, and through them, two eyes, opened wide, frightened, like a doe's paralyzed by the lights of an oncoming car. Mark stared back, locked in an invisible link, unable to turn away. Time stopped.

Again the light-studded blackness engulfed him. He knew his eyes were open — he could feel them stretching, his eyebrows lifting higher and higher, but the bleachers before him were gone and he was once again in that field. He'd wanted no part of what they were doing then. And he wanted no part of what they were doing now.

"Hey! What's with you? See a ghost?" Jake laughed, an ugly laugh. Mark jolted back to reality, but Jake was talking to Bunnie, not him.

Jake followed Bunnie's gaze. Spotting Mark, his face turned ominous. He didn't say a word, but the upward thrust of his chin, the flair of his nostrils conveyed a clear message.

Clutching the Cokes, Mark cleared out. A fight with Jake was the last thing he needed, least of all over Bunnie.

Chapter Three

In the dark, cold auditorium at Central High, a huge black grand piano sat in the spotlight, awaiting the next contestant. The pens of the four judges who were stationed in the middle of the second row, scratched and scraped over rating sheets. Scattered behind them, engulfed in the immensity of the cavernous room, were a few nervous contestants, piano teachers, and friends.

Mark slipped his arm around Becky, who was sitting ramrod straight, wringing her hands. "Relax, Beck," he whispered, covering her icy-sweaty hands with his. As she exhaled, he felt the tension ease, then constrict again as the announcer spoke.

"Next, Rebecca Jane Hargrove from Rolling Oaks High School will perform 'Rondo Capriccioso' by Mendelssohn."

"Relax, Beck. Enjoy it," Mark said softly. "Let the music flow through you." Becky took a deep breath and stood. She walked to the judges, handed them her music, then climbed the stairs to the stage. Mark felt his own shoulders tensing and forced them to relax. Maybe he could help, he thought, easing himself into a quiet state. *Let the music flow through you, Beck. Let the music flow*, he thought as Becky arranged the skirt of her teal blue silk dress on the piano bench. She sat quietly for a moment before she lifted her hands to the keys. *You are pefectly calm, relaxed. You will play well. The music will sing through your fingers.*

From the corner of his eye, Mark saw Harley leaning forward, acting more concerned now than he had for his own performance, which had been brilliant. Even the judges had leaned back while *he* played, forgetting to follow the handwritten manuscript.

Becky's initial attack was clear, precise, and steady. *That's the way, Beck,* Mark cheered silently. *Let it flow.* She sounded sure of herself, even as she sped toward the passage which had tormented her last night.

Harley's hands were moving to and fro, helping, too. Francine's fingers were crossed. *Easy does it, Beck. Let it flow. Let it flow.*

And then that terrible arpeggio rose and swelled under her touch, clear as a bell, without a single fumble or hesitation. Mark sank back into the seat's upholstery and closed his eyes, smiling. And suddenly he was back there again by the pond in the field after the Cub Scout family picnic. "Come on, Mark," Billy yelled, waving his glowing jar. "Grab one! You can catch 'em easy — they come right to *you.*" And then Billy had clapped his hands around one that was pulsing its light on a bush. Deliberately, monstrously, he pinched off the glow and smeared it, still glowing, across his forehead.

Mark shuddered.

The applause was spontaneous when Becky finished. Flushed and smiling, she stepped lightly across the stage, floating in a cloud of teal blue silk. She'd done a good job.

He and Harley and Francine followed Becky down the aisle, whispering congratulations, then huddled outside the door around Miss Parks, her teacher.

"That was marvellous, Becky!" Miss Parks was glowing, too. "It was the best I've ever heard you play."

"Great, Becky. Really nice."

"I'll bet you get a 'one' for sure," Francine said.

"I hope so." Becky wriggled her shoulders in anticipation. "You know —" she said, calming down, "— it was really strange. Once I got up there and sat down, I wasn't scared any more. It was like — like somebody was there helping me." She shook her head. "It was like the music just came through me and I didn't have to do anything."

"It *sounded* that way, too, Becky," Miss Parks said, giving her a hug. "Congratulations."

Mark stood back, watching, enjoying Becky's success, but wondering. "It was like somebody was there helping me." Had he done it? Had his thought messages helped? Was this — this mind power he seemed to be acquiring capable of producing a performance like that? And if so, what more?

"Well, Mark, you sure are quiet," Becky said. "Aren't you going to congratulate me?"

"You bet!" Mark smiled down into her sparkling brown eyes and pulled her to him, the light fragrance of her perfume caressing his senses. He felt her breath catch as his lips brushed hers. "Congratulations," he said softly.

"Ma-ark!" Becky pushed herself away, now more flushed than ever. She glanced self-consciously at Miss Parks. Mark laughed.

"Come on," he said; "let's go get some fresh air."

Outside, the mock orange and crabapple trees were in bloom. Harley squirmed out of his sports jacket and spread it on the grass for Francine and Becky. The four of them sat on the ground under an array of rose and yellow blossoms. Now all they had to do was wait for the ratings to be posted.

"Isn't it strange," Becky said, stretching and swishing her hair back and forth, "to think that all this will be over so soon? School. Seeing each other every day, doing all the things we've done for the past twelve years?"

"I'm ready." Harley said. "No regrets on my part."

"That's just because you already know what you're going to do next year," Francine pouted. "You wouldn't be so sure if you didn't have a scholarship and everything all set up for you."

"No sour grapes, Francine," Becky scolded. "You'll hear soon. You're bound to. Maybe you'll end up going to State with us." She flashed a smile at Mark, then turned back to Harley. "Aren't you nervous about going to Julliard? I mean, Julliard!"

Harley shrugged. "No, not really. Just about those New

York subways. What a maze. I'll be a-mazed if I don't get lost forever."

"Oh, boo!" Mark jeered. "Bad pun, Harley. Bad pun."

Harley shrugged again.

"Hey. I just thought of something." Francine said, clapping her hands. "You both will get to play for the Prom if you get 'ones'."

Mark squeezed Becky's arm. "That would be great," he said, thinking about Rolling Oak High's tradition honoring the highest-rated upperclass musicians by inviting them to perform during the intermission at the Junior-Senior Prom. "My date, the star."

"No," Francine objected. "*Our* dates, the star*s.*"

"I guess it would be okay," Becky said hesitantly, "but to tell you the truth, I don't really care if I never even *see* a piano again, at least not until next fall."

"Ha!" Mark laughed. "You'll change your mind about that soon enough."

"'Ones!' Both of you!" Mark whooped as he craned over the heads at the bulletin board. "All right!"

"This I've got to see for myself." Becky wriggled through the students bunched around their ratings. "Rebecca Jane Hargrove: 'one', she read, "Harley Amadeus Everston: 'one plus'. Harley," she exclaimed. " 'One *plus!*' "

"This," Mark proclaimed, "calls for a celebration."

"It sure does," Becky agreed. "Something wild and crazy and a million miles away from anything classical."

"How about Bo-Jo's burgers and germs?" Harley suggested, licking his lips.

"Ugghh," Becky groaned. "We always go there. I want to do something different."

"Like what?" Francine asked.

"Oh, I don't know. It's just that everything we do is so square. And I've been plopped in front of that dumb piano for so long I've practically grown to the bench. I want to do something fun. Something daring. And I don't have to be home to babysit Tye until seven."

Mark riffled through his mental list of places to go, things to do, and figured up quickly how much money he had left after buying gas for the car and lunch. He didn't know how much "daring" he could afford.

"I know!" Becky's face lighted up. "Let's —" she said slowly, eyes flashing, "— go — to — the — Arcade."

"The Arcade!" Mark exploded. "You've got to be kidding."

"She's been at the piano too long," Francine moaned, covering her eyes in mock dismay. "Her brains have turned into arpeggios."

"Hey," Becky bristled. "I'm serious. Why can't we go to the Arcade? I've never been there. They're supposed to have lots of neat games and a terrific sound system and —"

"— knifings, and drug busts, and gang wars —" Mark continued.

"At four-thirty in the afternoon?" Becky said, disgusted. "I'm sure. Mark, sometimes you act more like you're thirty-five than seventeen. Come on. Don't be such a bore. Let's go."

"Like this?" Harley said, looking at their clothes.

"Why not?" Becky was as prickly as a porcupine. "If we all go home to change, there won't be time to do anything."

As Mark drove toward the Arcade, he glanced over at Becky and shook his head. With the reputation the Arcade had, he'd rather never go there, but he supposed that Becky was right. Nothing much could happen at four-thirty on a Saturday afternoon. He turned a corner.

"Hey." Becky said. "What did you turn here for? This isn't the way to the Arcade."

"Oh." Mark blinked. Why had he turned? He hadn't meant to, hadn't been thinking about it. "Guess we're taking the scenic route," he said, shrugging. "I wasn't paying attention."

"Well, that's too bad," Becky sighed. "Look what's up ahead."

Mark was already looking at the line of cars slowly creeping out on the right shoulder of the narrow street around what looked like a wreck. "At least we're not in a hurry," he said sheepishly.

"I'm sure not," Harley grumbled. "I don't even like video games. They're so out of tune."

"Oh," Becky turned around to face Harley in the back seat. "It'll be fun, you'll see."

As Mark drew closer to the cause of the traffic jam, he frowned, and strained to see better. It looked like a stalled car with its hood up. A silver car.

"Melodic Mendelssohn," he exclaimed, "I think that's my mom!" As he drew closer and the sign on the side came into view, he knew he was right. He pulled back into the lane behind the Miller Rexall Drug car and cut the engine. They all piled out.

Mark's mom was standing in front of the car, peering under the hood, looking bewildered and helpless.

"Mom," Mark said.

"Oh, Mark!" Surprise and relief wiped the worried expression from her face. "You always show up at the darndest times. Just when I need you. The car stopped — no warning."

"Well, let me see — " Mark slid behind the wheel, turned the key. The battery growled, clicked, but was nearly dead. "You just need a jump, Mom, at least for now. The battery shouldn't be acting up on *this* car. Dad had better have it checked over."

While Harley stopped traffic, Mark manuevered the Fairlane nose to nose with the Marquis, and before long had it running again. "Better not stop before you get it home," he said, exchanging places with his mother behind the wheel. "Want us to follow you?"

"No. I'll be okay now, I think. By the way," she asked, "how did Harley and Becky do?"

" 'Ones,' both of them," Mark said, feeling more like a proud father than friend.

"Congratulations!" she called to them.

"Now we're off to celebrate," Mark said, purposely not filling in the details.

"Have fun. And thanks." She waved and drove away.

"Ma-ark," Becky said slowly as they started on their way, "why *did* you turn at that corner back there?"

"I don't know," he answered, shrugging.

"Doesn't it seem just a little strange to you that you just *happen* to turn at the wrong place and then just *happen* to find your mom who just *happens* to have had her car break down?"

"Uh-huh," Mark agreed. "It does."

Becky shifted uncomfortably in the seat, moving closer to the far window. "Mark, you're getting weird, you know it?"

"Not as weird as *you*," he retaliated, "wanting to go to the Arcade." But he had a strong feeling that finding his mom wasn't a mere coincidence.

Chapter Four

Mark pushed open the Arcade door and stepped inside. The odor of stale smoke assailed his nostrils as he stood blinded, waiting for his eyes to adjust to the dim light. Games buzzed and dinged from every wall, and new wave blasted over the sound system.

"Well, it's not classical." He turned to Becky, catching the wary look on her face before she hid it away.

"So," Becky said jauntily, "are we going to stand in the door all day?" She pointed to two games side by side across the room. "Let's try those."

There were games like the ones in the Arcade everywhere — in the mall, at the 7-11, even a couple by the vending machines at school, and Mark thought everyone had probably tried them at least once; but Becky never had.

"Well, all you have to do is put your quarter in." Mark dropped a coin in the slot, choosing the easier of the games, an old Pac Man, for Becky's first try. "The object of the game is to eat all the little dots with your Pac Man without —" he pointed to the four red, pink, blue, and yellow creatures on the screen "— your Pac Man being eaten by those ghosts first. This handle controls where Pac Man goes. Whenever you're ready, push the button."

Becky squinted at the screen, pushed the button and the chase was on, accompanied by the *woo-woo-woo* sounds of pursuit, all too soon followed by a little electronic tune that signaled defeat.

"Oh, no," Becky groaned, wrenching the handle too fast

23

and too far as Pac Man was gobbled up again to the music of the electronic ditty.

In almost no time, Becky's game was over. "You scored 1370," Mark said.

"Is that good?" Becky asked dubiously.

"Not very." Mark grinned. "At that rate, it would cost you about —" he calculated aloud. "— two games every five minutes make twenty-four games an hour would be — six dollars an hour."

Francine and Harley were playing Zaxxon. Mark and Becky watched a jet on the screen zoom into an enemy fortress, avoiding electronic barriers, rockets, and walls, only to explode into a flash of bright lights on the screen.

"Fun, huh?" Francine said, excited.

"Yeah. I want to play Pac Man again," Becky said, dropping a quarter into the slot, poised, ready and determined.

A skeletal demon with sharp talons glared through red eyes from a Space Invaders pin ball machine to their right. Something else there caught Mark's eyes, and he glanced over, at first seeing only the grotesque figure. But then he felt the adrenalin flitting through his body, responding involuntarily to what else he saw. Superimposed on the fang-like teeth and brown bones on the screen was the reflection of what was behind them.

"Becky," Mark said, moving closer to her, putting his hand on her arm.

"Don't!" She jerked away. The ditty played. "You made me lose."

"Becky, we have a problem," Mark said under his breath; then stepping in front of her, he turned. In a semi-circle behind them, five guys, uniformed in black leather and grease-stiffened jeans, had cut off their path to the door. Mark recognized the jackets. They were the same as Bunnie's and Jake's and Clay's, but more elaborate. And their hair —

"Well, well, well," one of them said, hooking his thumbs over his chain-entwined belt loops, thrusting his hips forward. "Lookee what we've got here." He had to be the leader. His head was shaved except for a long mohawk strip across the top, and long, long locks that hung to his shoulders in front of each ear. In the middle of his forehead was a small tattoo — some kind of symbol.

Harley and Francine turned. From the corner of his eye, Mark saw them looking to him for help. It was going to be up to him. Behind him the incessant electronic buzz of the games droned on and on.

"Don't seem very nice to have a real fancy dress-up party 'n not invite us," the guy said. "Spike" was embroidered on his black jacket. He dabbed into a round box and raked his finger inside his lower lip.

"Look, Spike," Mark said, trying to sound nonchalant. "What do you want?"

"Well —" Spike turned to his cronies, grinning. "Hows about an introduction to the little lady in the purty blue dress, for starters?"

Mark's stomach knotted. They were trapped, like Billy's fireflies. This had been a mistake. It was foreign territory. He'd have no chance in a fight — Harley, even less. He didn't dare antagonize them. Maybe talking would help, at least stall for time.

"Becky," he answered. "And I'm Mark." He hoped his voice didn't sound as scared to them as it did to him. "We're not having a party. Becky and Harley here —" He nodded over to where Harley stood looking as white as a marble statue. "— both played in the State Music Contest this morning."

"Well, ain't that nice?" Spike feigned sweetness to the others. "How's about playing for us, honey?" he said, leering around Mark at Becky. "I've got an instrument you can play." Then he nudged the guy beside him and laughed.

It wasn't helping to talk. Mark thought fast. "Speaking of playing," he said, choosing a tactic, risking it, "you guys know how to play this thing?" He gestured back at Space Invaders. "We're pretty green."

"You can say that again," Spike snorted. His audience snickered approval.

Mark reached into his pocket for a quarter, dropped it in the slot, then held out his hand in invitation. Spike hoisted up his jeans and swaggered over to the machine, legs spread. Mark gaped. Tattooed on the back of his head on either side of the swatch of prickley mohawk were two slanted staring eyes.

Slam! Pow! The balls rolled and Spike's whole body got into the action, hitting, leaning, gyrating against the machine. Mark watched as the focus of the others shifted to the game, then motioned to Harley and Francine, lifting his eyebrows and glancing toward the door.

"All right!" Mark exclaimed as Spike scored high. Harley and Francine edged away unnoticed. "You're really good at that." He squeezed Becky's arm, felt her trembling beneath his grasp, and eased away.

At the door, he waved. Only the blind tattooed eyes were looking.

Harley and Francine were in the car and the front door was open, ready for them. Mark heaved a sigh. "That was," he said, starting the motor, "not pleasant."

"Mark," Becky's voice was breathy, "I was so-o scared! How did you think of tricking them that way?"

"Well, they say 'necessity is the mother of invention.' " He was glad his heartbeat was finally slowing down. He wasn't nearly as cool as he was trying to act.

"Really, Mark." Harley clapped him on the shoulder. "Thanks for getting us out of that. I thought we were in for a fight for sure. Ohh —" he moaned, "my poor hands!"

"Well, Becky," Francine said, her voice caustic. "Was that 'daring' enough for you?"

"Hey, Francine," Mark frowned back over his shoulder at her. "Don't rub it in. All right?"

"I think I'd just like to go home," Francine said, now ticked off with him, too.

"Maybe we'd all better call it a day," Mark said.

In a strained silence, he drove first to Francine's house

and dropped Harley and Francine there, then stopped in front of Becky's. "I'm sorry, Beck," he said, reaching over for her hand. "We'll celebrate your victory another time. Just try to forget about the Arcade and remember the good part — how you played."

"Oh, Mark —" Becky's voice cracked. "I feel so — so stupid." Tears brimmed in her eyes. "It was all my fault, getting us into that mess. If it hadn't been for you, I don't know what they would have done to us." She sniffed.

"Come here," Mark said, pulling her toward him. "It was not your fault, only your *idea*. We *all* went." He held her close to him and wanted to keep on holding her forever. She seemed so small and vulnerable. "Becky," he said, nuzzling her hair, "you're really special to me, you know."

"Oh," she sniffed, "I don't know why. I'm such a dumb bunny."

"Hey!" Mark raised her head with the tip of his finger. "Don't talk about my girl that way. I wouldn't have a girl-friend who was a dumb bunny." But at the mention of that name, Mark again felt disturbed, uneasy, remembering the strangeness that seemed to have encroached on his life in the last few days, wondering again about the terror Bunnie was facing, apparently all alone.

Slowly, Becky's hang-dog look brightened into a smile. "You know, you're awfully nice, Mark," she said. "You could have gotten mad at me the way Francine did."

"*Me?*" Mark teased. "Get mad at *you?* Never."

"Well, I'm going to make it up to you," Becky announced, her voice bubbly and full of confidence once again. "Next Friday is your birthday. Right?"

Mark grinned, pleased that she'd remembered. "Yep."

"And I'm going to have one stupendous fun party for you. The whole gang will be there — Harley and Francine — if she gets over being mad — and Tom and Annie and Jackie and Bob and everyone. I already asked my mom and she even offered to help. And she promised to get rid of Tye, at least until his bedtime."

"Terrific!" Mark exclaimed. "I mean about the party, not Tye. He's not so bad, really."

"Not until he tries to be the center attraction at your party."

"Well, it'll be great." Mark said, feeling elated. "Thanks. I have to work all afternoon tomorrow to make up for today, but I'll be free by six. I've got some studying to do before Monday . . . maybe we could do something for a couple of hours."

"I'd love to," Becky sighed, "but my folks have invited all my relatives over for Sunday supper and to hear me play." Her voice dropped. "You could come —"

"Oh, no. That's okay, Beck. Really, I could use the time to study — I have so many things to do before graduation — and honestly, if I have to listen to "Rondo Capriccioso" one more time —"

"Yeah," Becky agreed. Mark was glad she hadn't taken offense. "I know what you mean."

"So I won't see you until Monday, then?" Mark asked.

"Guess not," Becky answered, then lifting her head, kissed him softly. "Thanks, Mark, for everything today."

Nobody was at home in the Miller House, except Napoleon. Mark found a note on the kitchen table. "Gone to pick up your Dad. He's taking me out to dinner. Casserole in fridge if you're hungry. Heat at 350° for thirty minutes. See you later. Love, Mom. P.S. Thanks for the rescue."

"Well, Nappy," Mark said, patting the old cat's head. "It's just you and me. Shall we make peace?"

Napoleon grumbled and stretched his neck out, inviting an under-the-chin scratch. Mark complied, then turned on the oven and stuck in the casserole. It was a strange feeling to be the only one home on a Saturday night. He flopped down in the easy chair in the corner to wait for his dinner. Napoleon promptly jumped in his lap, forgiving all.

As Mark let his hands slide over Napoleon's silky fur, his mind wandered back through the events of the last two days. First the experiments in English class, then that strange image of Bunnie's troubles, the people in cars, Dad, Becky's remarkable performance, "happening" across Mom's stalled car, the near catastrophe at the Arcade. All, Mark pondered, but the confrontation in the Arcade, had something very strange, something way out of the ordinary connected with them.

Some people were supposed to have psychic powers, and he'd heard about them but never paid much attention. It had always seemed like a bunch of unscientific voodoo — until now. Maybe Becky's performance was just luck, or Harley's coaching, but with Bunnie and Mom, he thought, growing more and more convinced; something *had* happened.

Napoleon's purring faded away as he twitched into sleep, and Mark's thoughts drifted into a daydream of Becky. He saw her again floating in the billowy cloud of blue silk. This time they were dancing. It was his birthday party and Becky was handing him a handsomely wrapped package, and he was saying, "Let me guess —"

Just then the buzzer on the oven jarred him back to reality and dinner. He pushed Napoleon off his lap and, suddenly famished, grabbed a pot holder and carried the steaming dish to the table.

Wonder what was in that package, he mused, laughing at himself for entertaining such silly fantasies. "I know what I wish she'd give me," he said aloud to Nappy, who was begging silently with his mournful eyes. "That green sweater with the white stripe across the chest that we saw at Sam's in the Mall last week."

I wonder, he thought, if I really did influence the way Becky played. I'll never know, unless — unless I do it again. What would happen if I bombarded Becky with some kind of mental message, like I did today? Something tangible, so I'd know for sure if it really worked, something like — He thought a few seconds, then laughed aloud. Something like a green sweater with a white stripe across the chest.

The idea, once conceived, grabbed his imagination so powerfully that he totally ignored the gnawing voice inside, warning that it might not be such a good idea. *Becky, ol' gal,* Mark concentrated, *for my birthday, I'd like —*

By the time Mark went to bed, he was feeling very devilish, his plan in full swing. He looked at his alarm clock, then chose a time — 3:33 — a bewitching hour if there ever was one — the perfect time for Becky to be susceptible to his suggestion.

I'll do it tonight. Again tommorrow night. Same time. Same station. Then wait and see.

Chapter Five

"Becky!" Mark called, spotting her walking toward school. He ran to catch up. "Hi," he panted, "top o' the mornin' to ya." He attempted an Irish brogue, tipping an imaginary hat.

"Hi," Becky mumbled. Mark slowed his pace to hers.

"What's the matter, Beck?" He looked more closely at the dark circles under her eyes.

"Oh, nothing. Just tired."

Mark cringed. He had carried through with the experiment. Could it have affected her like this? "Ah," he said, fishing for information, "didn't you sleep well last night?"

"No!" Becky snapped. "Or the night before, either. Maybe you were right about Music Contest. I got too uptight. And now I'm having a nervous breakdown or something."

"What on earth are you talking about?" Mark said.

"It's too weird," Becky said, pushing her hair away from her face.

"What? Don't be so mysterious." Mark had to know.

"Well, Saturday night, in the middle of the night I woke up. Just like that." She snapped her fingers. "I *never* wake up at night. Never!"

Mark swallowed hard. "What —" he said, putting his hand on Becky's arm, stopping her before they went inside the school. "What woke you up?" His curiosity pushed through the wave of guilt sweeping over him.

31

"At first I thought maybe I ate too much at the family dinner. But then it happened again last night. At the same time — just after three-thirty. I lay there all the rest of the night and couldn't go back to sleep. Like I said —" Becky gestured nervously. "— I think I'm cracking up."

"Did you tell your folks about it?" Mark asked. *He'd* gone right back to sleep and had slept well all night while Becky tossed and turned.

"No, not yet," Becky answered.

"Well," Mark sighed, relieved. "I'll bet you'll sleep all right tonight." *I promise,* he vowed silently.

The first bell rang, and Mark pushed open the door. Becky trudged in.

"See you in Sociology," he said. She didn't answer.

It was a good thing Mark didn't have a lot to do in his first hour study hall, he thought. He couldn't have concentrated. His mind whirled around the strange events he'd precipitated, struggling to bring logic out of the illogical; struggling, too, with the fact that he was to blame for the condition Becky was in today.

Whatever this is, it's like playing with fire. Mark stacked his books on the library table, got up, and walked over to the card file. *And I don't want anyone else burned because of me.* He scanned the alphabet to Pm-Q, pulled out the drawer and fingered through the cards. *Psychic. Psychic Discoveries Behind the Iron Curtain. The Psychic World of Peter Murkos. Psychic Self Defense.* He jotted down several numbers and went to the shelves, hoping no one would notice his choices, then pulled down a red-bound book, *Psychic Phenomena,* and glanced through the table of contents: "Strange Psychic Experience," "Paranormal Physical Phenomena," "Do All Humans Have E.S.P.?" He started to read, and a world — another dimension of the world than he'd known, began to unfold.

He didn't know how long he'd stood there, reading, but suddenly his single-minded concentration was broken. He looked up through the narrow opening in the stacks where he'd removed the books, and his eyes locked into another pair of eyes in the next aisle. Again. Those green eyes, lavishly outlined in black, stretched wide in shock and stared back, unmasking fear.

Shaking lose, he forced himself to blink.

Bunnie's eyelids fluttered. Furtively, she moved out of sight. Mark rushed to the end of the stacks and around the corner, but she was gone, nowhere to be seen in the library.

She'd run away, just as Nappy had. Am I so scarey? What? I look at people and they freak out, run away. What is it with me? He looked down at the red-bound book and tucked it under his arm.

In Sociology class, Mark slipped into the seat by Becky's. She looked awful, slumped on her desk, her head buried in her arms.

Maybe you should go home. He scribbled in a note and passed it to her.

"Maybe," Becky mouthed back, "at noon."

Sociology wasn't Mark's favorite class, but Mr. Moore made it impossible for him to be bored. This morning he began by talking about their final exam.

"Now, listen up," he said, strolling across the front of the room. "The final is this: to study any human institution in this community, visit it, interview people who are connected with it. By 'human institution' I mean school, hospital, church, Chamber of Commerce — that sort of thing. An organization that in some way serves the community." Mr. Moore stuffed his hands deep into his pockets and rocked back and forth from the heels to the balls of his feet. "I would especially like for you to choose something that really interests you, or disturbs, you, or makes you angry or happy — something you care about."

"How about the Bustop?" A male voice from the back of the room said. The class burst into laughter. The Bustop was a topless bar at the edge of town.

Mr. Moore laughed, too, and shrugged. "Sure," he said, "if you're old enough to get in."

"Between now and the final, acquaint yourself with the place you choose. Here —" he started passing out sheets of paper. "— are some questions and suggestions you might use. For the final — "he handed Mark a sheet, "— you'll write about what you've learned."

"You mean we'll write a paper for the final?" Becky asked, momentarily perking up.

"Exactly. I'm not concerned about typing and proper spelling and all that. I want you to spend your time *experiencing* whatever you encounter, then write it up during class. Okay?"

"Okay," came a few voices in response, while others, confused, had to have it spelled out to them again.

Mark wondered which of the institutions he knew about he'd choose. Community theatre? City council? Little league baseball? Nursing home, hospital? A creative final, he thought, glancing at the guideline. I approve.

Becky wasn't in Senior English, the other class they had together, and he hadn't seen her at lunch, either, but he had seen Bunnie. Before last Friday, he'd never seen Bunnie around school much, only in Senior English, but today he'd seen her twice in the hall and at lunch, besides that freaky peek-a-boo routine in the library.

His attention kept drifting to Bunnie during class, but he was reluctant to play around with his game any more. What if he was somehow doing something weird to Bunnie like he had to Becky? And he sure didn't want to read her mind again.

As he swung out of class into the hall, Jake and Clay slipped into his path, easing him back against the lockers. Jake had an iron grip on Bunnie's upper arm. She looked scared.

"We got a message for you, Miller — " Jake said, edging closer. A roach on a silver five-star leaf swung from beneath his shirt. "— from your friends at the Arcade. They think you must feel pretty smart, slipping out on them like you did, and they wanted us to tell you — if you ever come around again —" His eyes squinted nearly closed. "— they'll be *real* glad to see you."

"Hey, Jake, Clay —" These were the same flunkies he'd

been in school with for years. They'd never made it in anything. "Why are you getting mixed up with those creeps? They'll get you into big trouble."

"You're the one headed for trouble, Miller. Mind your own business!" Jake jerked Bunnie around, still glaring at Mark, then added, "You got the message."

Mark stepped away from the locker behind him and from the padlock that had been jabbing him in the back. So. He'd been threatened. He should be mad. Or scared. But it sounded like they hadn't planned to do anything to him unless he trespassed on their turf, and he had no intention of going back to the Arcade again, ever.

Becky wasn't in school at all the next day. During the break between classes he'd called her, but Mrs. Hargrove told him that Becky had come down with the flu and was sleeping. Guilt pressed down on him. It was his fault Becky was sick — he and his dumb experiment over a birthday party which they probably wouldn't get to have. To make his mood even worse, it turned cloudy and drizzled all day Tuesday and Wednesday. The week dragged by, a lifeless week without Becky, a disturbing week with Bunnie. He seemed to see her everywhere, all the time, like a mysteriously fleeting spirit, always disappearing, never speaking. And every time he saw her, he sensed fear.

Finally on Thursday afternoon Mrs. Hargrove agreed to let him come to see Becky and to bring her homework assignments. He was as nervous as he'd been on their first date, waiting to see her. He rang the bell, juggling the load of books and the dozen daffodils he'd bought on the way.

"Mark!" Becky opened the door and spotted the bright yellow blossoms. "How pretty!"

Mark looked at her, then turned quickly away, gulped in his breath and held it. He shouldn't laugh. He coughed, struggled back into control and faced her again. "How are you?" he asked, trying not to look at her hair. After all, he reasoned with his funny-bone which was again threatening to take over, she has been sick.

"Okay. I missed you." She took the daffodils and

pivoted around, then smiled mischievously. "And how do you like my new hair style?"

"Ah —" Mark gulped in air again. He smelled a trap. "Well, it's — ah —"

"— the latest!" Becky finished for him. "You dummy. You were supposed to laugh. I spent the last hour and a half getting it ready and you're too polite to enjoy it."

"You mean you did that on purpose?" He let his eyes sneak up to the clumps of hair that stuck out in every direction.

"Yes. One day I was lying here —" she plopped on the couch. "— and the TV was on, and I was so sick I couldn't get up to turn it off or change the channel or anything." She cringed. "Hate being sick. Yuck. Anyway, this stupid show about hair came on and a French stylist fixed a girl's hair — exactly like this. He used a machine that looked like a hybrid blow-drier and vacuum cleaner 'to create za most carefree style for za spring.' "

"It's carefree, all right," Mark said. "You look like you're standing upside down in a wind tunnel."

Becky's giggle was all it took to unleash all the laughter he'd gulped down. Instead of a nice laugh, though, it came rip-roaring out through his nostrils with a loud snort. That made Becky giggle even more, and that, in turn, got him even more tickled. Soon they were both holding their sides and gasping for air. "Shall I wear it like this to the party?"

"Oh, oh, no," he moaned, trying to stop. "That's the first time I've laughed all week. Beck, you *do* look fu-fu-" He looked at her hair and exploded into another fit of laughter which left him drained, sprawled on the couch by Becky.

Between sniffs and diminishing chortles, he regained his composure. "The party's still on then?"

"Of course! I had to get well for that."

"Good."

"So," Becky chuckled, picking up her math book, "besides not laughing, what have you done all week? What's been going on in school?"

"Nothing much. The usual." Getting threatened by a

bunch of thugs, but he didn't tell her that. "Work. I've been doing a lot of reading."

"About what?"

"Oh, just stuff." He couldn't tell Becky he was reading a book by an obstetrician who lives in a haunted house and believes in E.S.P. "Oh, she's fine," he said, "she said to tell you that she's sorry she got mad and that she'll call you about 'you-know-what.' "

"Mark!" Becky was looking at him with the strangest expression, her laughter all gone.

"What's wrong? You're not surprised, are you? Francine never stays mad for long. Or don't you know what 'you-know-what' is?" He chuckled, playing with the words.

Becky continued to stare at him and slowly pushed herself up off the couch. "Mark —" her voice sounded strained. "I didn't ask you about Francine."

"Yes, you did." Mark wondered if she was really over the effects of the flu after all. "You said —"

"No, I didn't, Mark. I was just *going* to ask and then you — you answered before I had a chance."

Chapter Six

Friday Mark awoke with a just-born feeling of freshness. The sunshine, almost painfully bright in the clean washed air, sliced through a week's worth of dreariness. Mark's gloomy meanderings into the world of psychic experiences seemed to evaporate with the beads of moisture that sparkled, then disappeared from the tips of leaves and blossoms. He was eighteen today. Becky was well again. He could feel it in his bones — everything was going to be okay.

Becky's return to Rolling Oaks High was like opening the first bottle of champagne at a wedding. She sparkled and bubbled from one friend to another, popping with excitement about the party. How could her energy level be so high after the flu? Mark hoped she wouldn't be a basket case by evening.

"Mark," she panted, rushing up to him at his locker. "You know you're supposed to dress up tonight, don't you?"

"Anything you say, m'dear." He grinned. "What are you going to wear?" He mimicked the way Becky and Francine had been talking. "I'd hate to clash." His humor was lost on her.

"My teal blue dress — the one I wore at Contest." Then a frown flickered across her face. "I hope you don't mind. I-I just couldn't get a new one."

"Mind!" Mark exclaimed. "I wouldn't mind seeing you in that dress every day. It's super." A fragment of memory flitted through his head — Becky in teal blue. He'd seen her wearing it another time besides at Contest, but where? He couldn't remember.

"Oh, Mark —" Becky squeezed his hand "— there's Annie. I've got to talk to her. See you in English."

Mark watched her dart her way through the crowd in the hall. He felt warm and lucky and special. Not many guys he knew had a girlfriend like Becky — a real *friend* girlfriend. The party tonight would be a highlight — for both of them. And, he sensed, the beginning of something new.

When Mark got home from school, he was surprised to see both cars in the driveway and wondered why his dad wasn't at work, especially since he'd given Mark the afternoon off. Curiosity whetted, he went inside. "Hello, everybody!" he hollered. "Hello, Nappy." He rubbed the toe of his jogging shoe over Napoleon's back.

The study door opened and both his mom and dad came out. Dad was holding a brown envelope. "Hi, son," he said. "Glad you're home. I was hoping to see you before the party."

His mom slid into her favorite chair, smiling mysteriously. Nappy claimed her lap.

"Have a seat, Mark." His dad settled himself on the sofa. Mark sat at the other end. "Well, this is a big day. You're eighteen. Hard to believe, isn't it, Janie?" He looked at Mark's mom and shook his head. "Well, you're probably wondering why there wasn't anything from us by your plate this morning."

He had wondered, it was true. Their family birthday tradition was to open gifts at breakfast time. "Yes?"

"Well, we weren't quite ready, but now — " He thumped the long official-looking envelope with his thumb. "— we —"

"I'll get it," Mark interrupted, reaching for the phone. "Hello?"

"Hey, Mark —" It was Becky, out of breath. "— bring your tapes tonight. Okay? Anything good for dancing."

"Okay."

"See you at 7:00." She hung up.

"Boy!" Mark grinned. "She is sure wound up." Then he noticed the peculiar looks he was getting from both parents.

"Mark —" His dad glanced at his mom.

"What?"

"Why did you answer the phone?"

"Why did I answer the phone? That's a funny question. Because I was closest to it, I guess."

"But, Mark —" His mother leaned forward in her chair. "— the phone didn't ring."

"Sure it did. It —" Then he stopped. *Had* it rung? He couldn't be sure. Yesterday Becky *hadn't* asked him a question, but he'd answered it. His earlier optimism plummeted from his head down through his stomach. It was happening again.

He leaned back on the sofa and covered his eyes with his hands. It was different when he was in control, just playing games, but this was too much. Now he didn't even realize when it was happening.

He felt the sofa sag. Mom was at his side. "What is it, Mark?"

Mark shook his head.

"Whatever is bothering you, son, you know you can talk with us about it. Anything." His dad was firm, powerful.

Mark looked from one to the other. "Look," he sighed. "I can't — I don't even know myself."

"The other day, Mark," Dad said, "at work, a lady came in. She was looking for something in the display case with all the lotions. She didn't say anything to you, but you reached for a bottle of Vitamin E Cream and handed it to her. You said, 'Here it is, Ma'am. Is there anything else?' "

"Oh, no!" Mark groaned. "It *is* worse than I thought."

"What's worse?" Mom asked gently. "Have other things like that been happening to you?"

Mark nodded and stood up, feeling smothered by their closeness. He stuffed his hands into his pockets and paced. "I never wanted to be a weirdo freak mind reader!" The words burst out with a vengeance.

"It's not too uncommon," his mom said softly. "It's not the end of the world. Some people have —" she paused, "a special talent. Maybe you're one of them. It's something you learn to live with, but —" her voice took on a tone of warning "— just remember that like all talents, it can be used for the good — or for the bad."

Mark had stopped pacing. This was his mom? He'd never heard her say anything about this sort of stuff before, but she *knew* something, he could tell. "Mom, have you —"

"Well, now —" she interrupted him, switching back to the way she usually was, as if she had turned off one personality and turned on another as easily as switching channels on TV. "Don't you want to know what your birthday present is?"

His dad handed him the long brown envelope.

Mark continued to stare at his mom. Did he know her at all? His own mother, after eighteen years?

"Well, take it," she scolded.

Mark fingered the envelope, trying to shift interest. It *was* an odd looking present — no wrapping paper, no frills. He slipped some documents from inside and unfolded them. A small card fluttered to the carpet. As he reached to pick it up, he scanned the page and realized what he was holding.

"Yahoo!" The war cry burst out of him unbridled. He couldn't believe his eyes, but there it was in black and white and legalese — the title to the Fairlane, in his name. "Wow, thanks!" he exclaimed. "Thanks a lot."

"The other paper is insurance — all paid," Mom added. "That card is your proof of insurance to carry in the glove compartment."

"Oh, wow. I can't believe this!" Mark felt firecrackers exploding inside. "Wait 'til I tell Becky!"

"Now, Mark —" Mom was in her Mom's voice again. Advice coming, he knew. "We trust you to drive carefully."

"And be responsible with the upkeep," Dad added, "*and* most important — our ulterior motive — come back to see us when you can once you've flown off to college."

"I will." Mark promised. "And I'll take good care of the car."

Mark wanted to blurt out to everyone that he had a car

— *owned* a car of his very own — as soon as he arrived at Becky's. He also wanted Becky to be the first to know. But she was busy, zooming into and out of the kitchen carrying last minute goodies down to the den. He'd break the big news to her later.

"Wait, Mark," Becky cautioned. "I want to go down with you." She stopped beside him, but he could still feel her motor racing.

Judging from the quiet roar coming up the stairs, Mark guessed she must have asked everyone else to come earlier.

"Okay, let's go now." Becky slid open the pocket door. "Here he is!" she shouted.

"Happy birthday, Mark!" came the chorus of greetings.

Mark laughed. Everyone had on tiny little pointed hats like they used to wear for birthday parties in first and second grade, the kind with little elastic chin straps, and they were blowing funny paper whistles. One unrolled into Mark's face, fluttering his nose with a feather.

"Becky," Mark shouted, "how did you ever do all this in one day?"

"It wasn't easy." Becky sagged, then bounced up. "Come on, everyone, let's eat."

A table full of sandwiches and goodies looked inviting under a canopy of twisted yellow and green crepe paper. In the middle sat a big decorated cake with his name and "18." "Did you do that, too?"

"Yep." Becky grinned, pleased with herself, then added, "with a little help from Francine."

Becky started the music and dimmed the lights. Soon everyone was dancing or playing Ping-Pong in the next room, or, like Harley, lingering over the food. The party was going to be an enormous success and Becky relaxed, abandoning her hostess role.

Mark opened his arms, inviting her to dance to the slow music he'd just slipped in the tape deck, and she floated toward him in a cloud of blue silk. They swayed comfortably, not afraid of touching too much or not enough. Dancing with Becky felt natural, right. He closed his eyes and drifted with the song.

An amplified click and the tape was over. "Hey, every-one," Becky called. "Time for presents and cake."

Mark's stomach puckered. Since Monday he'd tried not to think about Becky's present or that stupid experiment. He hoped, fervently hoped, it had failed. Regardless of what his mom had said, he didn't want that — talent.

As the presents appeared, silly stuff from the Ben Franklin or the costume shop, Mark's wariness wore off. "Ho Ho Ho," he laughed as he pulled some strange-looking cloth out of the package from Francine. Puzzled, he held it up and a big glass ruby caught the lights and flickered in its nest of white material. "What is it?" He turned it around in his hands.

"A turban," Francine said. "It goes on your head." She tugged it into place. "Like this."

"And *this* —" Harley handed him a strange comic-paper-wrapped shape "— goes with it."

Mark pulled the comics off a none-too-new water-lined fishbowl. "A fishbowl?"

"Nope." Harley took it from his hands, turned it over. "A crystal ball."

Francine's eyes sparkled mischievously, "For you — and your — power."

Mark cringed. It wasn't funny, his "power," but they didn't know. They were just joking around.

"What power?" Tom asked, and Francine told about Mark's amazing Mom-rescue.

"Weird, Mark," Tom said, "Does stuff like that happen often?"

"Oh, yes." Mark escaped into exaggeration — or truth. You're usually pretty safe with the truth. Nobody believes it. "All the time." He raised and lowered his eyebrows and stroked the air around his "crystal ball." "And now I shall tell *all*, about —" He turned and pointed his index finger menacingly at Tom's date. "— you!"

"Oh, Mark, cut it out." Becky grabbed his pointing finger, her twist a little harder than playful. She thinks I might do it. Mark reeled in the sudden crosscurrent of anger and absurdity.

Becky's eyes, her face, were suddenly different, painted over with a transparent protective layer. A cold chill shivered over the party. Mark's anger cork-screwed deeper. She should trust him, stop looking at him that way.

For an instant no one stirred; then Becky's voice broke through. "Well," she said, too loudly, "you haven't opened my package yet. I saved it 'till last." She handed him a brown and gold package with perfectly creased square corners, the pro-wrapped store type. Some fleeting recognition tickled his memory, but his capricious anger pushed it aside, pushed back at Becky's Nu-Skin covered face.

"Open it," she insisted.

Rondo Capriccioso, he thought, smiling a crooked smile. I can play it, too. He lifted his drooping fingers above the overturned fishbowl. His eyelids sank, and through the dark blur of eyelashes, he saw Becky's plastic cover tighten.

"No, *mon petit chou*," He kept his voice low, mysterious. "I shall instead, use the crystal ball." He closed his eyes. The room sank into a silence as deep as in Amenhetep III's tomb in its resting place in the British Museum that he'd read about in History.

A fleeting knife-point thought pricked his conscience — what was he doing?

"Ahhhhh —" He opened his eyes a slit, just enough to see pairs of unmoving feet. He was overplaying it, his eyes fixed on the fishbowl. "I see — I see an article of clothing. A shirt," he said quickly. "No, no," he mumbled, "not a shirt." He frowned, pretending deep concentration. "It's a sweater. Yes." Now rapidly, "A sweater — a *green* sweater with a white stripe."

Becky's Nu-Skin face molted. Shock, surprise then anger arranged and rearranged her expression. "Francine!" She whirled around. "I could kill you! You *promised* you wouldn't tell."

Francine threw up her hands. "I *didn't*. Honest!" Her eyes were wide. "I didn't even tell Harley."

Inside Mark's chest something cold, final, clunked, like the end of life — or youth. The experiment — damn it — had been a success.

Becky spun around, facing him now, clenched fists on her hips. "Then how did you know? Who told you?" Flickers of anger arced from the depths of her eyes riveting into him.

Stop it! The knife blade of guilt jabbed under his ribs and up, but Mark was already laughing. "Nobody! I *told* you —" He was crazy, a weirdo freak. *Stop it!* His stiffened fingers moved toward her, outstretched at face level. "I can read the crystal ball, *ma chérie.*"

"Oh!" Becky exploded. She crumpled onto a fluffy floor pillow. "It's not fair. I tried so hard to get just what I thought you wanted, and to surprise you and now somebody's ruined it!" She looked like she might cry in earnest.

One final fatal plunge. The guilt-edged knife severed the dissonance of Mark's perverted Capriccioso. He jerked the turban from his head and threw it down. The glass ruby clicked on the floor and scratched a trail of sound as it slid under the table.

"Oh, Becky," Mark felt like crying too. How could he have done that? He knelt beside her and gently touched her cheek. "Nobody's ruined anything, Becky. If it's the sweater we saw at Sam's it *is* perfect. And it *is* exactly what I wanted." He leaned over and kissed her lightly.

"Oooooo! Ahhh!" came the chorus of approval from the others.

"Honest?" Becky sniffed.

"Honest. Look." He sliced his fingernail between the edges of the shirt box and through the brown and gold wrapping, then reached through the tissue inside. *That's it all right. The verdict. Proof positive. Me. Mark Miller, weirdo freak.* He pulled the sweater on over his head and tugged it into place. "A perfect fit, Beck." He smiled, searching for forgiveness in her eyes. "Thanks."

"But —" Becky's mask was gone; confusion remained. "How *did* you know?"

"Lucky guess?" He'd hoped to bury it. But the smile he was trying failed. Something strong. Weights on the universal gym, pulling. Tendons at the back of his neck tensing tighter. Tighter. His head, creaking open, a fissure in an earthquake. *Have to go.* He struggled to his feet. *Have to go.* Had he said it out loud?

Looking at him funny. Everybody. Becky. "Have to go!" He'd spoken this time. He tripped. A pitcher on the refreshment table flooded its life blood onto the white tablecloth. Red encroached, slow motion, on the still undissected cake.

The fissure widened. *Go!*

Enshrouded in some all-powerful force field, a moth fluttering innocently toward the deathly luminescense of a crisp-fry bug lamp, Mark flailed helplessly up the stairs and out into the cold, mercurial blue haze of the street light. To the car. Unlock it. No! Back to the house. To the right. Left. Into the street. Running, running. Aware only of the call.

Chapter Seven

When Mark came to, he was wandering in an alley, out of breath, sweaty. It was dark. Late.

He had been at his birthday party — he shuddered — being mean to Becky. And then? He remembered the — what was it? — zap! It was like the first time in class with Bunnie, only ten times, a hundred times stronger. Something big was at stake. He'd had to help someone or else something terrible would happen.

But who? What? He hadn't done anything.

Mark looked up into the stars and shivered inside his new sweater, then followed the deserted black corridor out toward the lights. When he saw the street sign he fingered his keys wistfully. It would be a long walk back to the car.

The Hargroves' house had a put-to-bed look about it. Only a dim light shone somewhere deep on the first floor. The cars were gone, the party over. Poor Becky. He wanted to see her, to apologize. To explain, if that was possible, but he wouldn't dare ring the doorbell now. He stood on the front lawn staring up at her second floor windows thinking about rocks.

He was tired. Drained, as if somebody had directed a jolt of electric current through him, jiving him up momentarily, then dumping him, burned out, used up. His shoes cuffed the grass as he slowly turned to his car. He'd have to wait to see Becky tomorrow. And hope.

The car's dome light flickered on when he opened the door. His throat suddenly constricted. Air rushed backwards, groaning down his windpipe. Cocooned on his car's front seat was the shrouded form of a body.

Mark forced his trembling hand to reach inside. Between

47

thumb and index finger he plucked a corner and cautiously lifted it. Underneath lay familiar tousled black hair.

"Beck?" he whispered, trembling. "Beck?" He touched her shoulder.

"Huh?" Becky jerked awake and bumped her head on the steering wheel. "Ouch! Oh! Mark. You scared me." Mark's chest heaved, expelling air from its pressure tank. Becky sat up, pulling the cocoon with her.

"You scared me, too." He slid in beside her, clicking the car door closed as quietly as he could. He was certain the Hargroves didn't know Becky was here.

"I was so worried about you, Mark!" Becky's words flowed over him like a blessing. She wasn't mad after all. She reached for his hand and clutched it in both of hers, kneading it as she talked. "Are you all right? I had to know, so I sneaked out and waited for you here in your folks' car. You about had to come back here to —"

She was babbling. She did that when she was nervous. He removed his hand from hers and slipped his arm around her shoulder. "I'm okay, now, Beck. Calm down."

"Wh-what happened to you? Were you sick? The way you ran out of there, it was so weird! You acted like you were —" She was searching for a word. "— possessed!"

"It *was* weird." He pulled her closer to him. "I'm weird."

"What do you mean?"

"Well —" How could he tell her? How could he make her understand what he couldn't understand himself? He only knew he had to try. "You remember the other day when I answered your question before you asked it?"

"Uh-huh."

"Remember when I turned wrong on our way to the Arcade — and found Mom?"

"Yes."

"Well, a lot of strange things like that have been happening to me lately."

Becky pulled away and turned to see his face, hugging herself inside the snuggly.

"It's pretty hard to explain —" he began. He told her about the stare-downs in class — how it had all started, about Nappy and Contest and the telephone, but when he told her about the first zap, he didn't mention Bunnie. Intuition said no.

"You *what?*" He'd confessed too much. Becky was livid. "Do you mean to say that *you're* what made me wake up in the middle of the night?"

"But I didn't know —" Mark sputtered. "I never wanted you to —"

"You *experimented* on me like some laboratory guinea pig? You made me wake up. I got sick —"

"Beck, I'm *sorry!* I won't do it again, I promise."

"And I suppose that's how you knew about this." She grabbed the front of his sweater. "Playing around with my mind like some kind of toy. Ohhh!" She reached for the car door. "After this, you just leave me alone!" The dome light came on, illuminating her horror.

"Becky, please —" Mark didn't reach for her, not with his hand, but his voice pulled up from somewhere deep inside, pleading. "I'm in trouble with this, Beck. I don't know what's happening to me. I — I need you." He rubbed his hands over his eyes and leaned on the steering wheel, exhausted. The dome light — doom light — darkened. Becky's door closed.

"I — I'm sorry, Mark." Her voice faltered. "I was only thinking of myself — not you." Her cocoon slid across the seat and Mark felt her warmth encompass him. Her arms around his shoulders were giving, caring. "Please look at me," she begged. "Look at me."

Mark lifted his head from the steering wheel, felt its curve imprinted into his forehead. He was afraid to look at Beck. So tired. So sorry. Finally, he turned.

All anger had disappeared. Moisture shimmered on her lower lids, and now Becky's eyes, warm, searching, were reaching deep inside of his. Something clutched in his stomach. A strangled sound escaped from inside his throat. "Oh, Becky!" His arms went around her, pulling her to him with an intensity he'd never felt before. Words vanished.

Later, he didn't know how much later, he loosened his hold. "Thank you, Beck." He felt calmer, now, centered again.

"Nothing to thank me for." Becky straightened around and looked into his eyes. Something new glimmered in their depths — something beyond beauty.

"What am I going to do, Beck?" Mark forced himself to think again. "I can't stand this crazy psychic stuff zooming in on me and taking over whenever it gets the urge. It's out of control."

"Do you really think —" Becky pushed the words cautiously as if they were dangerous — "it — ah, — comes from outside you?"

The question was like a slap. Mark jerked. He hadn't even considered otherwise. But if it didn't come from outside, then — "But, I'm not making it up!" he exclaimed. "I'm not crazy! Psychic, maybe, but not crazy."

"Mark, Mark, take it easy," Becky soothed. "I didn't say you were crazy. It's just — well —" Her voice suddenly was stone hard. "I just don't believe in this psychic business." She rushed on. "I think you've just got to make yourself stop dwelling on it. Stop experimenting. Just act like a normal person again, okay? No more weird books. No more freaky stuff. Okay?"

Becky made it sound so wonderfully easy. And it was exactly what he wanted — to be normal again. And who knows? Maybe he was — courting — these, these, whatever they were. "Okay," he agreed, feeling better already. "Starting right now, I am normal. Do you hear me, universe? I AM NORMAL! I will not have any more weirdo freakouts."

Becky laughed. He took her hand. "How about a normal date with a normal guy to a normal Sunday night movie?"

"I'd love it." Becky entertwined her fingers with his and squeezed. "With Harley and Francine?"

Mark shook his head. "Not this time. This time I want

you all to myself." He thought beyond the movie to the mountainside overlook above the Rolling Oaks Valley, and being alone together watching fireflies. "Oh —" Suddenly he remembered. "I haven't told you yet. This is *my* car. My folks gave it to me for my birthday."

"They did?" Becky exclaimed. "Mark, how wonderful. Your own car. Now I like you even better than before." She grinned at him and ducked away from his teasing fist.

"Out!" He commanded, pointing to the door. "Out of my chariot!"

But Becky moved closer instead. "Do you really want me out?" she said, lifting her eyes to meet his. Her long lashes fanned over her cheeks as she closed her eyes and tilted her head back. Mark's heart thumped hard; then slowly, his head floating, he let himself be drawn closer and closer to her. Their breath mingled. Lips touched, softly, timidly — at first. But then, something else happened. Becky gasped. Her eyes, shocked-surprised, opened wide, a little scared, mirroring Mark's own turmoil.

Shakily, unable to resist, they blended again. Mark's hand, suddenly possessing a will of its own, found its way inside the snuggly, needing to touch. Wanting.

"Oh, Mark," Becky sighed. She clung to him even more tightly.

Something profound, something new was happening to them. And, Mark realized, something dangerous. He was fighting for control over urges that always before had been less demanding, more private. He was getting uncomfortable.

"Oh, Becky, Becky." He forced himself to surface from the agonizing bliss. His hands moved to her shoulders, pushing her gently away. "You've got to go inside."

"I don't want to," she murmured. "I don't ever want to." She tried to snuggle back against him. "I just want to stay here with you."

"But Becky, don't you see?" Mark held her away, fighting himself, fighting her. The throbbing was getting worse, threatening embarrassment. "This could get away from us."

"What?"

"Oh, Beck, don't you know anything?" He was really hurting now. "Sex! Becky, sex." A slow look of recognition washed over her expression, then a wave of fear. "I love you," Mark said, pleading. "That's why — you've just got to go in the house. Now. Please!"

Chapter Eight

Ever since "Googoplex" hit the box offices, everyone had been saying it was Academy Award caliber, better even than "E.T." and "Star Wars" and "Close Encounters," but as it moved past the too-long string of credits, Mark couldn't agree. It wasn't going to be that good, but it didn't matter. In fact, it would be kind of nice to be only mildly engaged. He stretched back in the reclining seat, enjoying the movie for what it was, enjoying being with Becky, enjoying life — everything — more than he had for a long time. Nothing strange had happened to him all day.

He snatched a handful of Becky's popcorn — his was all gone.

"Hey!" she objected, then grinning, snuggled close to him. His arm automatically found its place around her shoulders. Something like a huge bubble pushed up at his Adam's apple, threatening to burst from too much happiness.

He poked into the bottom of Becky's popcorn box. Nothing but old maids were left. He spread his fingers inside, lifting it away from her, and dropped it on the floor, then settled back to pay attention to the screen.

He might have been nearly asleep. Later he tried to remember. He had been at least close enough to sleep to have lost the story line when it happened. No earthquake-slow fissure this time, no wrenching universal gym. A sharp dead ringer, on target. A clean shot. It was, in fact, quite simple. Almost natural. A voice — a female voice — in his head. "Mark, help me. I need you," it said. Like an announcer interrupting the music in earphones, the voice slipped into his mind, taking precedent over everything. It didn't occur to him not to go. Everything else, even Becky, paled in comparison.

He leaned over. "I'm sorry, Beck," he said, "but I have to leave." That was all he said. He stood, calmly, as if he were on any ordinary trip to the men's room, and slid past the knobs of knees to the aisle.

Outside the theater the sharp evening breeze brought him up short. So now what? There was no doubt in his mind who the cry had come from, but where was she? Where was he supposed to go? And somewhere in the back of his mind, the question — And why me? I don't even know her.

He looked wistfully back at the theater. Beck would be furious. If he'd go back in now, he could smooth things over. If not —

The second wave hit. No voice. Feelings. Their intensity flashed terror through his mind. He decided. Becky would be okay, but Bunnie — Bunnie needed him — now.

He pivoted on his heel, grabbing the keys from his pocket, and ran to the car. Gravel spewed as he pulled out, too fast — driving, he realized, sweat breaking out on his forehead, directly toward the Arcade. How? Why? He didn't know — *couldn't* know, but yet he knew. That was where he had to go. He felt the sweat turn cold under his arms, down his spine. The Arcade.

Flashing raw yellow bulbs outlined the front of the square building and the letters A-R-C-A-D-E, but theirs were the only lights. The sides of the building and the back parking lot were dark, purposely so, Mark thought grimly, clenching his teeth as he pulled into an empty space next to an undulating van with a dim interior light glowing through bubble windows. As he squeezed out of his door, he turned quickly away from the activity in the back seat of the car at his side.

Well, Bunnie, he thought, here I am. I hope we both get out of this place in one piece. He turned up his collar, stuffed his hands into his pockets, and trying to disguise his fear, forced himself to saunter past the back door and around to the front entrance.

Sweet blue smoke and dim lights from the video games and pin ball machines, the indistinguishable sound of loud blasting music punctuated by cracking whips and electronic beeps and dongs, the clack of balls on pool tables, consumed the people within, made them seem unreal, multishadowed throwbacks to some cave existence. Mark suppressed a cough as he slid along the wall, half turned, trying to be invisible. Again his clothes were a dead give away. A survey of the room from the corner of his eye confirmed his worst fear — lots of black leather and *that* hair cut.

He scrunched down into his collar, stiff shouldered, and began to inch his way behind the players and around huddled groups, avoiding eye contact. His breathing was shallow. The stuffy smoke-filled air tickled his throat, courting a coughing spell. The tingle of adrenalin raced through him. Across the room he spotted Clay, but Bunnie wasn't with him. Jake, either. If Bunnie is here, he thought, I'd better find her soon, before someone finds me.

At Mark's side a machine blatted defeat and a spew of filthy words and irate energy splattered over him. "Stupid — machine!" The player slapped it with the palm of his hand, then spun around, crashing into Mark. "Watch where you're going, chump!" he yelled, pushing Mark aside.

The taste of copper flooded Mark's mouth. He dived into the vacated machine, burying himself between its wings. His heart pounded in his ears. That was all he'd needed. Had he been seen? He dropped in a quarter and faked playing, waiting. The back of his neck prickled. Was he being watched or not?

When he finally turned, his knees, suddenly weak, threatened to buckle. He was staring into those unblinking tattooed eyes. He caught his breath. He was really in trouble — *bad* trouble. Should he try for the door? Spike was talking. There were three of them intent on something he couldn't see. Spike's hand reached around into his back pocket and fished out a wad of bills.

If he moved, he might draw attention to himself. But if he waited — He didn't have a chance to decide.

"Snoopy, ain't ya?" a gravely voice said over his shoulder, moving in close. Mark's knees turned to water. "You're pretty dumb for a narc, if that's what you are," the voice said without emotion. "Move."

Mark moved, plastered against the hulky body behind him, deeper into the bowels of the Arcade. Spike didn't look up. Nobody did. Mark scanned the room frantically, panic edging closer and closer to the surface. If only he could spot Bunnie, maybe she — but she still wasn't with Clay. Then, like a non-feeling robot, his brain began to calculate. I'll go along with this until I get back away from the crowd, and then I'll — He didn't know what yet, but he'd do something.

He was being pushed into a smelly, toilet-paper strewn back hall. There were three doors. A sign hanging crookedly on one read, "Broads," the other, "Studs." The third door had to lead outside.

Bunnie! Suddenly, he knew where she was. It wasn't another zap, just intuition. He knew! "Look, pal —" Holding out both hands, palms up, he pivoted, facing his captor. He *was* one of them — black leather, the hair cut. "— you've got it all wrong. I'm no narc." His computer was whirring. So far, so good. At least he hasn't clobbered me yet. "I didn't want to make a scene out there. Look man, my —" He couldn't say "girl"; the guy might know her, "my sister is sick in there." With only the instant's hesitation it took to break an ingrained taboo, he moved, fast. "Bunnie!" he called, then pushed open the door to the women's room and barged in. And there she was.

Her startled face was tear-stained and blotchy, with an ugly patch of purple over one cheek bone. She stared at him, mouth open, unmoving.

"Come on," he whispered urgently. "Let's get out of here."

"How did you know?" she gasped. "How did you find me? They'll kill you!"

"Come on!" Mark grabbed her wrist and led her out the

doorway, past the black leather jacket, toward the back door.

"Hey!" The voice shot out behind them. As Mark pushed on the door handle, he glanced back. A quick motion — the silver flash of a blade.

Bunnie saw it, too. "It's okay, Kahn," she said. "See ya."

Kahn vascillated. Outside, Mark grabbed Bunnie's hand and ran. "My car's over there." He unlocked his door and nearly pushed her in, then slid in beside her and locked the door. Kahn and Spike, with several others, piled out of the Arcade and descended on the car, yelling.

Mark floorboarded the gas pedal. Tires squealed. "—get you for this, Miller!" someone yelled.

He glanced at the rearview mirror and saw the swinging chain. He'd been lucky. It could have gotten the car — or him.

Several blocks away he eased up on the accelerator and made himself lean back into the seat. He was as tight as a new fan belt. All his chemical forces had gathered at the front line to defend him, but now they weren't needed. Like soldiers after a warning drill, they were revved up for a battle not to be fought. Mark could smell his own metallic fear.

Bunnie didn't say a word, but as he calmed down and shifted his attention to her, he could see she was in bad shape. Her body was trembling all over — shudders racked her in waves from her shoulders to her feet again and again.

Mark eased the car around a corner out of traffic, down a quiet residential street, and parked under a proper-looking Colonial style gaslight in front of somebody's home.

"Bunnie," he said softly, turning sideways, accidentally touching his knees to hers. "Bunnie, what were you doing at that place? What happened to you?"

Chapter Nine

In the silence, Bunnie's shakes subsided. She held herself, arms hugged tightly across her chest. Under her eyes, mascara was flaked and streaked until it was hard to distinguish where the bruise began and the make-up ended. Mark watched her, waiting. "You — you don't have to tell me," he said cautiously. "I — didn't mean to be —"

Bunnie glanced over at him with those frightened green eyes, then looked back at her hands. "It's okay." He could barely hear her. She let out a long quivery sigh. "H-how did you find me? How did you know?"

Mark leaned back, breathed deeply. *For two weeks, you've never been far from my mind. Everywhere I've gone, you've been there. Every place I've looked, I've met your eyes. My mind, my life, is somehow connected with yours.* But he couldn't tell her any of those things. Instead he asked, "Bunnie, did you want me to help you?"

Her head ducked low, then slowly, she nodded.

"But why? Why me?" Mark blurted.

"I — I don't know. I — I thought —" Her breath hitched. She was almost whimpering. "Somehow, I felt you were a decent person, that somehow — you — you *cared*." She was crying now, rushing on. "I'm sorry. I had no right. You don't even know me."

Mark impulsively reached out, gripping her shoulder. She flinched, like a dog accustomed to abuse. He lightened his hold, still touching her. "I do care, Bunnie. Tell me, who hit you? What's going on?"

Strands of Bunnie's long hair buried her face. He couldn't read her expression. "Jake," she finally said, almost in a whisper, then again her shoulders began to shake. "H-he's a beast. An animal!"

"So why do you run around with him? It doesn't make sense, Bunnie, with what he's done to you. You're a nice girl —"

"Ha!" Her expletive was bitter, caustic.

"You *are!*" Mark insisted. "I don't mean what you've done. I mean who you are inside. You're a good person. It's just that you're in a bad situation."

There were tears in Bunnie's eyes when she looked at him. Encouraged, he ventured on. "Why don't you make some new friends? Stay away from *them.*" He was sorry as soon as he'd asked. Bunnie gave him such a knowing, sympathetic look that he felt like an idiot.

"What do you think would happen," she said softly, "if I walked up to your Becky, or Francine or Annie, and said, 'Hi! I'd like to be your friend'?"

Mark's throat tightened. She was right, of course.

"I made my mistake when I first came here. I chose my 'friends.' "

"Well, how about meeting new people in a church group? Or maybe talk to a school counselor?" He blundered on.

"Oh, Mark," she said, not harshly, but with a quiet resignation, "you don't understand at all. You couldn't."

"Well, maybe not," he said, fighting a growing sense of frustration. "So, what *do* you want?" He stole a look at his watch. The movie would be over about now.

She crumbled. "Out! I want out! Away from Jake and Clay and —" She shuddered. "Away from everybody. Everything." He'd never heard anyone scream in such a soft voice before, as if she was used to being afraid of being heard. "But I'm trapped. I'll never get away."

"Can't you talk to your folks about it?"

"Ha!" That bitter laugh again. She flung her head; her hair flipped against Mark's face. "Fat chance. I can't even be at home. My mother —" she said it like a dirty word — "is too busy with her boyfriends — if you want to call them that. If I'm home, some of them forget who they've come to see."

Mark stared, aghast, slowly understanding.

Bunnie sighed. "You-you're a nice guy, Mark," she said sadly. "You live in a different world from mine."

Mark nodded. "I guess I do, but Bunnie, you don't have to stay in your world if you don't want to. Maybe I am naive; maybe I don't know all the sordid details of your life, but I believe you are in charge of what happens to you. You are the one who decides to let it happen."

Bunnie's face showed nothing. Neither acceptance nor disbelief. "Are you in charge of your life?" she asked flatly.

"Yes," Mark affirmed, driving his point home. "I am."

"Well, I'm sure not. I'm just a Ping Pong ball battered back and forth between people who control me, and none of them care anything about *me*."

Through her misery, Mark heard the echo of his own voice bouncing back at him. *Yes! I am!* Heat crept up from under his shirt collar. Was he so sure? If he was in such good control, why was he here now? Had this been his decision? "Bunnie," he said, "I'm sorry. I sounded like a pompous know-it-all just then. To be honest, I don't know if I'm in charge of my life right now or not. I still believe that I should be."

They both sat, absorbed in private thoughts. A car cruised by and pulled into a driveway. Doors slammed. Voices.

After a long lull, Bunnie looked at Mark again. "Please don't take this wrong." Her voice was like a feather, barely brushing the air. "D-do you feel something — for me?" She rushed on to say, "I-I don't mean romantically, just something. Some kind of — of link?"

Mark gulped.

"Oh!" It was a sound of exasperation, frustration. Bunnie hid beneath her drooping hair once more; then in a near whisper she said, "I shouldn't have said that. Now you probably think I'm crazy."

"I don't think you're crazy at all," he replied, but his

head was whirling. What if Bunnie had been having the same things happen to her? What if she'd been reading *his* mind? Suddenly he felt naked, vulnerable. "And yes," he said, tentatively, "I do know what you mean about the link."

He could hear her — a long sigh. "You do?" Incredulity laced her voice; and for the first time, the fear in her eyes was replaced by a flicker of hope. "You do?"

"This is strange. I mean, really strange, isn't it?" he asked, feeling a growing closeness to a kindred spirit, someone who might really understand. "H-how can we talk about it?"

Bunnie's eyelids fluttered. In a barely audible tone she asked, "Do you think about me a lot?"

Mark nodded.

"Since when?"

"Two weeks ago Friday," he said.

"Me, too." Bunnie's excitement was creeping into her voice. "Before that I knew who you were, but I never paid any attention to you, and then —" She ducked her head, as if she was uncomfortable with talking so openly.

"Go on," Mark urged.

"All of a sudden, it was like you jumped into my mind. I was so — so desperate, I needed someone so badly, I tried to convince myself I was just fantasizing escape, but at the same time, I *knew* it was more than that. You were everywhere. And —" she looked out the window, her voice trailing off — "I felt so ashamed, as if you somehow knew everything about me."

"Bunnie," Mark asked, "do you read my mind?"

"Oh, no!" She turned, surprised. "No, it's not like that at all. It's just — well, after you first — appeared —" She touched a finger lightly to her forehead. "It was like I had someone to turn to. I'd think about you and — and wish. I guess I saw you as —" She laughed lightly. It was the first time Mark had ever heard her laugh. "— my knight in shining armour, coming to rescue me. And —" she added, "you did."

"Something bad happened to you Friday night, didn't

it?" Mark seized onto an idea, calculating the zap at the party. "Sometime around ten?"

The pupils of Bunnie's eyes dilated, then shriveled into pin-pricks again. She nodded.

"You thought about me then — and tonight, right?"

Again she nodded.

"I knew, or sensed, that you were thinking about me. I got your message. Tonight, I even heard your voice inside my head, and somehow — don't ask me how — I knew where to find you."

"I — I" Bunnie sighed. "This *is* strange." She ran her fingers through her hair, pulling it back away from her face. "Has it ever happened with anyone else?"

Mark shook his head. "Not like this."

"Why us?" She was whispering now.

"I don't know," Mark said. "I don't know."

"For me," Bunnie said softly, "I'm glad. I haven't talked to anyone — *anyone* — this way since I moved here. Nearly two whole years. But —" She let her hair fall back into place. "I'm sorry, too. You don't know what getting messed up with me could mean. Jake and Clay and those other guys —" She was clutching her arms around herself again. "— especially Jake — They're not as dumb as they seem. They'll get me for this. And you."

Chapter Ten

Becky avoided Mark all the next day; but now, as everyone jostled into Senior English, he was waiting for her. "Becky!" He reached out, but she dodged, nearly colliding with, of all people, Jake.

"Oh!" she exclaimed. "Excu-u-u-use me, Jake." She smiled up at Jake, ignoring Mark completely. "I should be more careful where I'm going." Mark's insides coiled.

Jake puffed up like a blowfish. "That's okay, Becky." He shot Mark a dark look of triumph over Becky's head. "You can run into me any time you like. Any time."

High-wire tension shot through the three of them, forking, crackling through the air.

"Take your seats, please." Mrs. Bethune short-circuited the mounting hostility.

"I guess she means us." Becky tossed the words over her shoulder and swished to her desk. Even her voice was not hers. She'd taken on an almost southern belle accent for this performance. Mark crashed into his seat, hard. He could understand why she was mad at him, but she didn't have to act like this. He felt like yelling or shaking her or throwing a book at her rigid back. He also wondered what had happened to Bunnie. Why wasn't she here?

The class finally ended and Mark bolted out of his seat. "Becky —" He grabbed her arm. "Don't run off." Then lowering his voice, he said, "You have a right to be mad —"

Becky glared at him. "Yes. And I am. Now let me go!"

She wrenched her arm away from him and her stack of books sailed off the notebook in her arms and splayed across several desks and onto the floor. Neither stooped to gather them up.

"Becky, please, at least talk with me. Give me a chance to explain." Mark fought to keep his voice to a whisper. Mrs. Bethune was watching them from the front of the room. Everyone else had gone.

"We can't talk here. Come on." He started picking up books. "Let me buy you a Coke."

Becky's shoulders dropped a hitch from their defensive position. "All right," she said dryly.

They settled into a booth at Bo Jo's. Neither had said a word on the way. Mark decided not to mention her scene at the beginning of class. Some things are best forgotten. He leaned across the table toward her. "Becky, I apologize. I'm sorry. I —"

"What can I get you two?" It was Jeanne, a girl from their Sociology class, now dressed in a blue checkered uniform.

"Two large Cokes, please," Mark answered. "Becky, would you excuse me for just a minute? I've got to make a phone call."

"Sure," Becky said, flippantly. "Who to? Bunnie?"

She knew about Bunnie! Mark kept his voice level. "To my dad. I'm going to be late to work."

When he slipped back into the booth, the Cokes were there, and Becky was staring down her straw into the sparkling liquid as if escaping into another world. "So what do you know about Bunnie?" he asked.

"Oh, nothing," she said, sarcasm rising through her voice. She stabbed her straw through the ice. "Except that you dumped me at the movie last night to late date her, and everyone in school is talking about it."

"Becky! That's not what happened at all!"

"Oh? You weren't parked with her in front of Annie's neighbor's? Annie *saw* you."

Mark groaned. This was sounding like a stupid soap opera, and getting worse all the time. "No. No." He shook his head. "Not *parked*, not what you're thinking. We were talking, that's all —"

"So you *were* with her!" Becky exploded, evoking giggles from the next booth. "Everybody knows what she is. She's nothing more than — than a —"

"Beck!" He stopped her. "Lower your voice. Everyone's looking at you." Then calmly, deliberately, he said, "Bunnie is in a lot of trouble. She needs help."

"You bet she does!" Becky flared.

"Okay, okay. Let's start over. This isn't getting us anywhere." This time Mark told it all, from the very beginning and the first mind-zap in class with Bunnie. Becky's expression, while she listened, changed from stony anger to fear and confusion.

"But, you promised, remember?" she said weakly. "You said you'd forget about all that weird stuff. Mark, it's just too spooky. It scares me."

"And me." Mark reached across the table, cupping his hand over Becky's on the laminated wood. "I don't think I can ignore it. It just — happens."

Becky looked down, pulling her hand from under his. "I think you make it happen. You want it to happen. You've spun out into this weird orbit and you're high on it — Luke Skywalker of Rolling Oaks High out to rescue our local Princess Buxom Bunnie."

"Becky, please!" Mark winced. "Don't call her that. She's a *person*."

"So am I!" Becky snapped. "Not a worm, and that's what I felt like when I had to call my dad to come after me at the show. You're not real popular at my house right now, by the way," she added.

"Oh, Becky." Mark cradled his head in his hand. "What more can I say? 'I'm sorry?' I've already said that. Becky, you are the most wonderful person in my life — everything we've done together, our friendship, and all that we *will* have — more than either of us knows. What I told you the other night is true. I don't know what's going on with me right now, but I need you to stick with me." She wasn't looking at him. "Last night I didn't mean to hurt you. That 'call' came and I —" He started to say "had to go," "— *chose* to go. Somehow I knew that you would be okay, but Bunnie — she needed help. From me."

Becky finished her Coke, then looked up. Sadness filled her eyes. "Mark," she said, "I care about you, too. I really do, but I don't know if I can handle this." She ran the tip of her finger over his hand. "I'll try."

But the way she said it was somehow scarier to him than when she'd been really angry. "Well. Enough heavy stuff." He worked up a grin. "What do you say?"

Becky's smile spread slowly. "Somebody did once say, 'Life is too beautiful to be taken seriously.' "

"Who said that?" Mark challenged, playing.

"I don't know. It's a rough translation of the Japanese characters on Tom's T-shirt. Must be true."

"Ah, so." Mark bowed. "In that case, I propose a chocolate ice cream sundae topped with marshmallow and chopped peanuts. You game?"

"But what about work?"

"Ah, so," Mark said, trying to sound oriental, "an-shant Japanese T-shirt say, 'Rife too beautiful to take seliously.' Jeanne, bring us two sundaes — chocolate ice cream with marshmallow topping, chopped peanuts and a cherry. And two more large Cokes. It's pig-out-on-sugar time."

"You can say that again. How will I ever eat dinner?" Becky giggled, her old self again. "Mom will kill me."

"Becky —" Mark changed the subject. "— have you decided what you're going to do for the Sosh final?"

"Yes." Her eyes lighted up. "The Oak Valley Journal. I've always been fascinated by the newspaper world. It's going to be fun to have an excuse to nose around in it."

"Sounds good." Mark nodded. "I'm doing mine on the nursing home."

"The nursing home!" Becky turned up her nose. "How morbid. Why did you choose that place?"

"I'm not really sure," Mark said. "It took me a long time to decide, but I was there every day for a week when I was in fourth grade, delivering papers for Harley while he was at music camp. It made a real impression on me." He remembered the crumpled people in wheelchairs, the smell, the shining polished floors, and the cat. Somehow the most human thing about the place was that black-and-white striped cat that roamed the halls and belonged to everyone. "Have you seen my cat?" Every day he was there, one old lady had asked him that. "Maybe if I go again, I'll get a better perspective on it. I wonder — Dad let me have some time off for this tomorrow — would you go there with me after school?"

"Sounds depressing," Becky said.

Jeanne set the sundaes and Cokes in front of them.

"Well, well! Look at this, would you?" Francine's voice burrowed into their space. Mark and Becky looked up, surprised. "But I don't know why —" Francine glowered at Mark, " — after what *you* pulled. May we join you?"

"Sure," Mark had to say. Francine was already sliding in beside him.

"Bring me one of those, too," Francine said as Jeanne returned. "Oohhh fats city!"

"No." Harley was shaking his head. He sat gingerly on the bench next to Becky. "Just a small glass of milk, please."

"Well, I don't know what happened," Francine went on, "but I'm sure glad you two are back together. I was scared to death everything would be messed up for the Prom after all our plans and everything."

"Have you been practicing, Becky?" Harley asked. "You are going to play, aren't you?"

Becky shook her head. "Right now, I'm not even sure I want to go to the Prom."

"Not go?" Francine screeched. "Why not?"

"Oh —" Becky shrugged. "It's just, well, with all this weird stuff that's been happening to Mark, everything we do gets ruined. You saw him at my house."

"Yeah." Francine rolled her eyes. "Far out!"

Mark felt as if he weren't there, like a kid being talked about at a parent-teacher conference.

"What *is* going on with you, Mark?" Harley asked, looking intently at him over the top of his glasses.

"I wish I knew."

Harley fished for something in his notebook, pulled out a flier, and held it up while the others read. "I don't know." Harley shrugged. "But I thought if I were in your shoes, I'd want to know what was happening to me. Maybe you'd learn something at this. Maybe not." He shrugged again. "We could all go and see."

"It wouldn't hurt anything," Francine said. "I'm game. How about you?"

Becky frowned. "I don't know. I just don't like this — any of it."

Mark was studying the flier, reading more carefully this time. *Psychic Exploration*, the title said. *"Extra sensory perception is an ability everyone possesses. This presentation will cover basic techniques to assist in developing and learning to use, at will, extra sensitive abilities."* His focus dropped to the bottom of the page. *"Dr. Pat O'Reilly is a noted psychic, lecturer, and faculty member of the Institute for Psychic Exploration."* "I don't know, either. I think anybody who advertises himself this way must be some kind of quack — a circus side-show type." But he was touched by Harley's gesture of concern, and intrigued by the words, "at will" on the flier. "I guess we could always leave if we don't like it."

"Okay by me," Francine said. "Come on, Becky. Say you'll go. Mark went to Music Contest with you. It wouldn't hurt you to go to this with him."

"Well —" Becky looked reluctantly at Mark. "If you promise not to embarrass me or do anything weird, I'll go."

"I promise, Beck," Mark said, holding up his right hand. "I'll be good. But right now, I'd better get going, or Dad'll be putting up a Help Wanted sign."

Chapter Eleven

Valley View Nursing Home looked exactly the same to Mark as it had when he was ten. The floors still shone like glass and the air carried that same odor, as if the windows had not been opened in the past six years.

He stepped up to the administrator's open door and tapped lightly. "Hello," he said, "Mrs. White?"

"Oh, hello." A very large woman who somehow reminded him of an Army sergeant glanced up at the clock, then stood. "You must be Mark Miller."

"Yes, and my friend, Becky Hargrove."

"Hello, Becky. Come in and sit down; tell me about this project of yours."

Mark explained the Sociology assignment and, scribbling notes in his notebook, asked the question he'd prepared, adding and revising as she answered. "How do people feel about coming here?"

Mrs. White sighed. "Usually, at first, not good. They come here because they have to. Most of them would rather be at home, but often they don't understand or remember that they can't take care of themselves anymore."

"You said, 'at first.' What happens after they've been here awhile?"

"They get used to it, usually. Sometimes, after they go home with their families for a weekend, they can hardly wait to get back here. We had one — " She was interrupted by a bump at the door, and Mark turned to see a nice-looking gentleman with sparkling blue eyes and shiny silver hair. His wheelchair had bumped the doorjam.

"Yes, Fred?" Mrs. White asked, waiting patiently.

It took Fred a few seconds to speak his thoughts. "I need to get back down to the bank to finish up that loan agreement. Please call a taxi, will you?"

"Fred," Mrs. White said, "you are in the Valley View Nursing Home now. You were sick, in the hospital, and now you are in the nursing home. Go back and watch TV or talk to Charlie. The girls will be around with some juice for you pretty soon."

Fred's chair bumped again. "Thank you," he said, rolling away.

"How sad," Becky murmured. "He reminds me of my grandfather."

"It is sad," Mrs. White agreed. "I knew Fred when he was the president of the First National Bank. He was a brilliant man." She sighed. "We can't change what's happened. We can only work with people the way they are now. Well —" She stood. "You asked for a tour. Mary Ellen, one of our nurses' aides, has agreed to show you around. If you'll wait here a minute, I'll find her for you."

After Mrs. White left, Becky whispered, "How can people stand to work in a place like this?" She shuddered. "It's so depressing."

"I guess somebody has to do it," Mark said, but he was feeling it, too.

Mary Ellen, a girl not much older than they, led them through the living room, the dining area, and kitchen, then down a long wide hall with residents' rooms on either side. Each door was decorated with a sprig of paper spring flowers and the names of the residents. Some of the rooms were full of furniture from home — easy chairs, TVs, big high poster beds, pictures and knick-knacks — while others were sparse.

"This —" Mary Ellen pushed open an extra-wide door — "is the tub room. That's a hydraulic lift. We put the patient in the chair and it rises up and swings around —" she motioned above a deep box-like tub — "and goes down into the whirlpool. It sure saves our backs."

"How often do the people get a bath?" Mark asked.

"At least once a week. More often when necessary."

Once a *week?* Mark looked at Becky, saw her look of disbelief that reflected his own feeling. No wonder the place smelled the way it did.

Mary Ellen moved out into the hall again. "Would you like to meet some of the people?"

"Yes, please," Mark answered while Becky shook her head.

"Paulda —" Mary Ellen raised her voice. "May we come in? These two students from the high school would like to meet you."

"Oh, yes. Do come in, my dears," the creaky voice replied. The tiny lady with a bright grannie-square afghan over her knees peered up at them. "Oh, my!" she exclaimed, "such nice-looking young people! What are your names?" She reached out and took Mark's hand in hers. Her skin, like a leaf of lettuce, seemed so fragile that it might tear, but there was still surprising strength in her grasp.

"M-Mark," he replied, feeling small, somehow, in her presence. "Mark Miller. I'm glad to meet you, Paulda."

"And I'm Becky Hargrove," Becky added politely.

Paulda smiled up at them, as if sharing a special secret for which words were not needed. "Good," she said, squeezing Mark's hand. "Good."

"I'll show you one more room," Mary Ellen said; "then I have to go. We're short-handed today." Then raising her voice, "Thank you, Paulda."

"You come back and see me again," Paulda said, releasing Mark.

"The man by the window in this next room," Mary Ellen was saying, "had a double-sided stroke during surgery three years ago. He has been totally paralyzed ever since."

"Totally?" Becky parroted.

"Well, almost. Sometimes the big toe on his right foot moves, but that's all. He can't eat. He can't talk. He can't walk or sit up."

"How tragic," Mark said. "He's been that way for three years?"

Mary Ellen nodded.

"Can he — does he — think?" Mark asked, trying to grasp what it would mean not to; or maybe, even worse, to be able to think, but not talk or write or do anything.

"Well, we don't know for sure. His wife comes and sits with him every day. She talks to him and asks him questions. *She* believes he responds to her by wiggling his toe, but that's only wishful thinking. The movement is a reflex action; he has no control over it."

"How terrible." Becky hung back as they approached the door. The name under the yellow and pink flowers was John Talbot.

Mary Ellen bustled over to his bed. "Hello, John." She checked a plastic bag of brownish colored stuff that hung over him and ran through a tube that disappeared beneath his bedcovers. "This is John's dinner," she said.

Mark's stomach turned. There were other bags and machines all around the bed.

Just then another nurse came into the room. "Mary Ellen, can you help me with Annabelle?"

"Okay," Mary Ellen said, already leaving. "Feel free to look around all you like. Do you have any other quick questions?"

"Is the cat still here?"

"Oh — Tabby?" Mary Ellen laughed. "He's our oldest resident. Yes, he's still here. He owns the place."

Alone with Becky in the room with John Talbot, Mark felt uncomfortable, like a trespasser, looking at a man who was not able even to prevent people from looking at him. John Talbot lay in the bed, facing away from them. He didn't look old. His hair fringing the balding spot was a sandy color. And his skin was pink and smooth and puffy-fat, like a baby's skin before it has been exposed to the sun. His backside was uncovered and a lamp was shining on some painful-looking red sores.

"Mark," Becky whispered, "let's go."

He didn't know why he said no, except that he was still trying to sort out his feelings. What would it be like to be John Talbot, lying there for three whole years? If I were in his place, how would I feel about us standing here staring at *my* exposed backside? Shouldn't I at least say something to him, acknowledge that he is a human being?

Mark swallowed hard, then walked quietly around to the other side of the bed where he could see John's face. "Hello, John," he said. John's eyes were open, but Mark couldn't tell whether he could see him or not. "Ah, the nurse told me that you had a stroke — a — a long time ago. I know you can't talk, but maybe you can listen, so I hope it's okay with you if I talk for a little while." Then he couldn't think of anything to say. What was he doing, anyway? He glanced over at Becky, who looked pale and fidgety.

"Ah," Mark floundered. "I know you're name is John Talbot. My name is Mark Miller. I'm a senior at Rolling Oaks High School. My girlfriend, Becky, is standing over by the door. Come on over here, Becky."

She looked terrified, but she came tiptoeing around the bed and stood at Mark's side. "H-hello, John," she said, her voice a little squeak. "It's nice to meet you."

What could he talk about? The sociology assignment? Why he was here? Hardly! What if John could understand? It would be like saying he'd come to study the monkeys in the zoo and that John was one of the monkeys.

"John?" Mark asked, on an impulse, "can you wiggle your toe?" He watched the covers at the end of the bed, but his right foot was under the left and he couldn't tell if he'd moved it. Feeling like a thief — he had no right to be doing this — he gently loosened the blankets and lifted them away from John's feet.

"Mark," Becky exclaimed in a whisper. "You shouldn't."

He ignored both his own internal warning, and hers. "Now I can see your toe, John. Can you wiggle it?"

He stood, waiting, staring at the pink toe with its too-long nail. "If you can move it, John, we can try to talk to each other." He waited again, a long, long time, but when the response came, it wasn't because John had wiggled his toe.

"Oh — my — God," Mark said slowly. Firefly pinpoints of light darted across his vision. Mark blinked them away and forced himself to look from John's feet up to his face. "Becky —" He turned. "He-he does! I almost understood him. John. John! Just then you said — you *thought* something — real strong. Do it again."

Mark's pulse was racing. He felt as if he'd been running, out of breath. He closed his eyes, breathed deeply and exhaled slowly, clearing, clearing, clearing away thoughts, feelings — clearing away even the wish to communicate. He waited.

"Mark," Becky whispered. "Have you gone crazy? What are you doing?"

"Nothing. Please, be quiet." His system, revved up by her intrusion, once again had to be mastered. It had been so close, like Bunnie's almost-received message the night of the birthday party. Only then he hadn't known what it was. Now he did.

What would it be like to communicate with another human being again, after three whole years? No. He insisted, urging his mind to release the thought, release everything, drift.

He didn't know how long he'd waited when it happened. He didn't know whose voice it was — John's or someone else's — but the words he heard were John's. "Let — me — out — of — here."

Mark blinked, aghast. John was paralyzed, hooked up to tubes and machines everywhere. "But, John," he said aloud, looking into the unfocusing eyes. He heard Becky, huddled by the window, gasp. "What do you mean? Out of bed? Out of the nursing home? How?" He was shivering. This was crazy. This was what he didn't want to do — sink deeper into this psychic darkness — and now he was doing it on purpose. He leaned over John again. "Think your answer to me. Think it strong."

It was harder this time, nearly impossible to calm himself, especially as he sensed Becky's anxieties reaching a *ff* at the end of a crescendo. "Becky," he said, opening his eyes and turning to her. "This is not hurting anything. Maybe it's helping. Please, just a few more minutes. Try to calm down, okay?"

Becky only stared back. The thought flitted through Mark's head that at least, seeing *this*, she could hardly still believe that it was just something he made up.

"John, think it strong."

The darkness that first covered Mark's eyes danced with specks of color and wiggly moving lines, then ebbed into blackness. He breathed deeply. Tension flowed off his shoulders. Intermittent random thoughts, words, flicked through his mind — maybe John's — but disconnected, meaningless. He sank further into the stillness, until from there, somewhere, not as a voice, but a gently formed thought, the answer came to him. *John wants out — of his body.*

Like an elevator on high speed, Mark shot dizzily to the surface. "You want to die!" he exclaimed.

Suddenly, something started to happen to John. Choking, coughing, something. Horrible sounds, strangling sounds, rattled through the phlegm in his throat and he was gasping, gasping for air, his head jerking involuntarily.

"Nurse!" Mark ran into the hall, yelling. "Nurse, help!"

Two nurses came running toward him.

"It's John — he's —"

They were at the bed. One grabbed a long plastic tube and stuck it down John's throat. It started to make a sickening sucking sound.

"I think you'd better leave," one nurse said icily.

Becky fled into the hall, but Mark backed away slowly. "Good-bye, John," he said. And in response to John's last unspoken plea, he promised, "I will."

The nurses stared at him as if he was insane.

Becky sat huddled in the car as Mark eased under the wheel into space that felt as if it was marked Keep Away. "Beck —"

"I don't want to talk about it," she snapped. "Please. Take me home." Her jaws clenched closed again.

Mark studied her frozen expression, then sighed and looked away. His head, his emotions, were too much a jumble with what had just happened with John to push through another closed door now. "Okay," he said, starting the car.

Chapter Twelve

Mark grabbed hold of a rough scrub oak. His knee, already muddied, burrowed into the ground, pushing as his arms pulled him up and over the ledge. He stood, panting, and turned to look back down.

He'd reached the top of the mesa overlooking town and now he let his focus wander over what looked like the kindergarteners' Lincoln Log village. Below him was the school. He'd needed to get out of it. To think. To be alone. So he'd left. His books, his homework, his car, all abandoned in the school lot. It was the first time he'd ever ditched.

He could see kids, like the dots on Pac Man, spotting the football field near his car. The hedge that bordered the school parking lot from here was a heavy outline. And there was his house, and Becky's. On a clothesline in their neighborhood something bright orange waved like a flag signaling to him. Then, on a rise on the far side of the valley, he saw the red brick and glass of the Valley View Nursing Home.

Behind him on the fresh green of the flat-topped mesa a meadowlark warbled. Its song was pure, bell-like, simple. Mark turned and walked on. How had his life become so complicated? Worry now taunted him constantly — worry about losing his marbles with this psychic stuff, worry about Bunnie and her messed up life and how he could help her, worry over his disintegrating relationship with Becky, and missing work so much, and finals, and all there was to do before graduation, and now — John. He felt caught up in an avalanche of events that threatened to dash him into a million pieces.

He'd become obsessed by John, and by what seemed to him to be a responsibility that was his alone — to be John's only link with the rest of the world. It was so awesome — what happened with John, and Mark didn't know anything about it — about strokes or wanting to die or *that* kind of E.S.P. It was a far cry from playing around with a stopwatch in English class.

He followed a ravine down toward a strip of trees, crawled through a barbed-wire fence, and picked his way through a small field of colorful rocks, glacial rocks, he guessed, from the way they were rounded. At the center of the draw, a tiny sparkling stream leapt down hill, over tree roots and rocks, gurgling and singing. Mark sat down on a boulder, watching the sunlight sparkle on the splashing beads of water, listening.

He was almost afraid to let go anymore. Sometimes it was when he relaxed, when he was off guard, when inside he was calm and centered, that messages came to him — and he didn't need any more messages. But the lulling water touched his turmoil, and despite his resistance, he began, gradually, to feel at peace again.

From his memory he heard himself — his own wisdom — reaching out to him. "Water symbolizes life — the underlying, sustaining presence of life and the assurance of renewal and hope." "Go with the flow, Becky. Let the music flow through you." "This is not hurting anything. Maybe it's helping." Pictures, like a multimedia slide show of the past three weeks flashed before his eyes, a kaleidoscope of feelings.

So, he thought, scooping up a handful of sand and letting it run slowly through his fingers, maybe I'm like Becky, slamming at the arpeggio, trying to force it to be right when all she had to do was to let it flow. Maybe my 'music' is, like Mom said, this "talent" to be in tune with other people and just to be there to help however I can. Maybe I just have to accept that I really am a weirdo freak mind-reader.

But this time, those words didn't make him mad. In fact,

he felt a lot better, as if he had reached as high a plateau inside as he had on his climb. The sadness still remained, though, deeper than any he had ever felt. He knew that sooner, or later, it would mean losing Becky.

Chapter Thirteen

Mark was surprised that Becky even came. He suspected that Francine and Harley had pushed her into keeping her promise, or maybe she just planned to tough things out with him until after the Prom and graduation, then call it quits, all their plans for being together at State U. in the fall, cancelled out. Even though she sat beside him, there was a transparent barrier between them. His arm, no longer automatically cradling itself on the back of her chair, felt out of place resting on his leg.

Francine had chattered incessantly ever since they'd left, covering the tension. Mark stopped listening to her and looked around the room. It was a small, off-beat church, and the meeting was to be here in the sanctuary, a pleasant area with lots of green plants and one beautifully crafted stained-glass window which hung away from the wall with a spot light behind it — the best they could do, Mark guessed, without any outside windows. It was certainly different from the huge Episcopal church his family attended downtown. He smiled to think of folding chairs in their sanctuary instead of the plush padded oak pews; still, there was a nice feeling about this small room. Aside from Becky, Francine, and Harley, he didn't recognize anyone in the mostly middle-aged audience, but they looked normal enough, the kind of people he'd see at Safeway or at his folks' bridge club. A stir in the back of the room made him turn to see a laughing man, obviously the center of a group, come in.

"Good, good!" He clapped his hands together. "What a

nice gathering. Good evening, everyone," he said, walking through the space between the chairs. Mark tried to check his immediate liking for the man. Wait and see, he warned himself.

"I'm sorry to be arriving so much at the last minute," the man said. "My plane was delayed and we only just landed —" he glanced at his watch and shrugged — " a few minutes ago."

"Well —" He passed the two chairs that sat facing each other on the podium, and stepped behind the lectern. "I'm Pat O'Reilly." He smiled. The flier had said *Dr.* Pat O'Reilly, Mark remembered. At least he wasn't pretentious. "I've come to talk with you tonight about the world of extra-sensory activity. Some of you here could probably easily give this talk for me. Others of you may only be discovering or acknowledging experiences that seem to reach beyond the ordinary. I hope there will be something of value for all of you, wherever you are on your journey."

Mark was aware that Becky was watching his reactions from the corner of her eye.

"Ever since Jesus walked and taught on this earth," Dr. O'Reilly said, "we have known that people learn best through parables and demonstrations, so I will begin with a few of the latter." He drew a packet of cards from his coat pocket and fanned them out. "These are simply colored cards — red, blue, green, yellow — There's no trick to the exercise I'm about to do with them." He shuffled the cards and stacked them, colored sides down, then closing his eyes, he placed his finger tips on the top card. "This card is blue." He turned the card. It was blue. "Yellow." He flipped the second card. "Blue. Red. Yellow. Green. Green." He was always right.

Mark glanced around Becky and Francine to Harley. Harley shrugged, obviously unimpressed.

"For you skeptics," Dr. O'Reilly said, opening his eyes, "I assure you that these cards are not marked, and I'm not 'peeking.' " He grinned. "It is a matter of sensitivity and practice. Each color gives off a different vibration, and my fingers, in communication with the deeper-than-conscious mind, know that difference."

Becky seemed to be interested, and not too uncomfortable, as Dr. O'Reilly proceeded with other demonstrations. "Now," he said, grinning again, "you are supposed to be impressed with all that, so now you will listen to the rest of what I have to say."

The audience laughed. Mark wondered what was coming next. Thus far, there wasn't anything here to explain what was happening to him, or to help him with a girl in desperate trouble and a man who wanted to die.

"How many of you have ever had premonitions? Feeling or sensing somehow that something extraordinary was about to happen?" Mark turned to see lots of hands go up, Francine's among them.

"How many have had the feeling that you have been in a place where you *know* in reality you have never been before? You already know somehow that the bathroom is down the hall, third door on the left."

Again, there was laughter and hands went up in the audience.

"Well, these experiences are tiny scratches on the surface of the possible. Einstein, Jung, Sagan, and many others, have all spoken of the untapped potential of the human mind, and they are so right. We all have repressed and unrecognized abilities that are not acceptable to the logical scientific mind — of the world's or our own. Sometimes we call extraordinary experiences coincidence or luck, but is that what they really are?"

As the lecture delved into a more serious vein, Mark found himself leaning forward, straining to understand a strange new vocabulary and the concepts it expressed. "— in communication with universal consciousness." Dr. O'Reilly paused, then leaned over the lectern.

"You know," he said, his voice taking on a lighter tone. "I'm really *not* a freak. I'm no different from your local D.J. except that he works in the communication field with radio equipment, and I work without it."

Mark laughed and looked at Becky. She was laughing, too. Their eyes met and the old look of rightness was there again. Mark reached for her hand. Becky smiled and squeezed.

"Psychic readings have a bad reputation —" Dr. O'Reilly was switching gears. "— séances, haunted houses and witchcraft, and fraudulent set-ups to relieve old ladies of their money. There is more to it than that, though, and tonight — not for the spectacle, but rather — and this is important — for the sake of demonstrating that we all are one, united in a deeper than conscious level, I will do a reading on someone from the audience, someone I have never met before. Could I have a volunteer, please? Someone I don't know."

The room became silent. Becky tensed. Mark wondered what was coming next. Was this what he'd been doing without knowing it? Psychic readings? Was that the same as mind reading? He wished Harley or Francine would volunteer so he'd know it wasn't a set-up. He felt an excitement welling up inside — the promise of an explanation, maybe a way to help Bunnie and John and himself, and to finally feel he was back in charge of his life again.

Dr. O'Reilly was frowning. People were shifting in their chairs and those with their hands up were looking uncomfortable. What was taking him so long to choose?

"No," Dr. O'Reilly said. He gestured downward with both hands, like a minister seating his congregation. "Put your hands down, please." He stood quietly a moment; then in a soft, kind voice, he said, "There is someone in this audience who needs very badly to talk with me. Will he come forward, please?" He was looking straight at Mark. His eyes were warm. He seemed older now, almost fatherly, and he was encouraging him.

"No!" Becky whispered, "don't!"

With no fear, without any reluctance, Mark stood. Becky was still clinging to his hand. He looked back down at her, yesterday's sadness recurring. He had to go his own way.

"Yes, young man —" the psychic said, "— Mark, isn't it?"

Mark nodded. Somehow it didn't seem strange that he knew his name.

"Please come on up, Mark."

Mark walked up to the podium.

"First, Mark, for the benefit of the others — Have you ever met me before?"

"No," Mark answered.

"Have you ever done or seen a demonstration like this before?"

"I — I don't know," he answered as honestly as he could.

"That's okay," Dr. O'Reilly said, then he pointed to one of the empty chairs. "Now, if you will sit there, please, I'll sit, too. I want you to answer the questions I ask with yes or no. You will not be hypnotized. You are in no way under my power. You are perfectly free to answer as you like. There is plenty of time. We don't need to rush. Are you ready?"

Mark nodded.

"Okay. Remember, answer with yes or no." Dr. O'Reilly settled into a comfortable position. He was breathing deeply, slowly. His eyes weren't closed, but they seemed to be seeing something far away. He didn't speak.

Mark glanced out into the audience. Becky looked up-tight, but Francine and Harley both seemed to be intrigued by what was going to happen.

"Mark —" Dr. O'Reilly's speech was different, slower now. "Are you a student?"

"Yes." That one wasn't too hard to figure out.

"High School?"

"Yes."

"Uh — something Oaks? Roaring, no, Rolling. Rolling Oaks High School?"

"Yes." He could have known that, but if he just flew in —

"Are you a senior?"

"Yes."

His questions were coming faster now, his voice more

secure. "And do you also have a job in — some kind of store?"

"Yes."

"A drug store?"

"Yes."

"Oh!" Dr. O'Reilly smiled. "It's Miller Drug Store and you're Mark *Miller*. You work at your dad's store after school."

Mark said, "Yes," even though it hadn't been a question.

"Do you have a girlfriend?"

"Yes."

"Does her name begin with a B?"

"Yes." Mark glanced at Becky and grinned.

"B. Is it —" he paused; "Bunnie?"

"No!" Mark nearly shot from his chair. Becky's face turned bright red.

Undaunted, Dr. O'Reilly continued. "I'm getting two names, Bunnie and Becky. You do have a special relationship with this Bunnie, don't you?"

"Yes." He wanted to say, "but she's *not* my girlfriend!"

"Hum." A muscle twitched over Dr. O'Reilly's eyebrow. He shifted in his chair.

"Are you taking a sociology class?"

"Yes." Mark relaxed back into his chair. Thank goodness Dr. O'Reilly had started a different line of questions.

"Do you have to do something unusual for the final?"

"Yes."

Dr. O'Reilly frowned. His head was turned as if he were listening to something he couldn't quite hear. "Do you know a man named John?" he asked slowly.

Mark tensed. "Yes." Goosebumps shot up on his arms.

"From Cedar Run?"

Mark opened his hands, palms up. "I don't know." Is John from Cedar Run? If he is, Dr. O'Reilly isn't just reading my mind. He can't be, because I don't know.

There was silence for a long while. Mark felt himself getting hot and sweaty. He began to wish he'd never agreed to do this.

Mark —" Dr. O'Reilly leaned forward, looking at him intently. "I'd like to talk with you about your questions," he said softly, "but not here. Will you stay so we can talk later?"

"Yes," Mark agreed, feeling relieved, "I'd like that. Thank you."

"Thank you, Mark," Dr. O'Reilly said in a public voice. "Now —" He stood. "— would someone else come forward?"

"Boy! Was that freaky?" Mark whispered, leaning across Becky to see Harley's and Francine's reactions, too. "He was right about everything." Then remembering, he glanced at Becky, and quickly glanced away, his ears flaming. "Almost," he added.

"But why me?" Mark heard himself whining like a grade school kid. "I'm only a senior in high school. I should be taking finals and throwing water balloons and getting ready for the Prom and graduation. How am I supposed to know anything about this stuff?"

"Mark, Mark," Dr. O'Reilly soothed. "Age has absolutely nothing to do with it. Those thoughts — those images that come to you are ageless. Sometimes you may surprise yourself, sounding like a wise old man, but you are merely a channel. A vehicle. You, Mark Miller, don't have to *know* anything. You just have to learn to stay out of the way."

"This is too much!" Mark's head was pounding. "Who's going to listen to me?"

"Anyone — Dr. O'Reilly said, smiling calmly, "who hears through you their truth."

"But —" He didn't have another argument.

"Listen, Mark, you will hear your own voice speak that which you cannot 'know.' Listen, and learn, and grow within your own soul. You will have a wonderful life."

Becky, Francine, and Harley had waited for him while he and Dr. O'Reilly talked in another room. Maybe he understood things a little better now, but he felt disappointed that the understanding wasn't going to make things any easier, maybe even more difficult. Practice, he'd said, to master using it at will. Practice, and time. He was disappointed, too, that Dr. O'Reilly wouldn't go with him to see John.

"It's all right," he'd said. "You can handle it. John needs you right now and he needs release. You can help him understand that it is all right to move on." He paused a moment, reflecting, then added, "Or it may be that someone else is holding him here, consciously or unconsciously willing him to stay alive. Perhaps you can help whoever it is to understand that it is all right — in fact, good — for John to move on."

"But how?"

"You'll find the way," Dr. O'Reilly said calmly.

"So —" Francine broke into his thoughts, "— what did he say?"

"To see John again," Mark replied, looking not at Francine but at Becky. "Will you go with me. Please?"

Becky's eyes misted over and she ducked her head, shaking it slowly. "I know I should, Mark. I feel sorry for him, but that stuff you do — it — I-I just can't."

"It's okay, Beck." He knew it was true. She couldn't. He reached over where she was huddled next to the car door, to touch her. "It's something I have to do myself."

Chapter Fourteen

The last frenetic week of school was even worse this year with graduation and pending freedom. Some teachers nonchalantly dismissed seniors from finals while others demanded more from them than ever — a final retribution for escape. The sociology final — Mark's last — was scheduled, college-style, in the 9-12 slot Friday morning, and he wanted to honor his promises to John and Dr. O'Reilly before writing it. Since he didn't have any afternoon tests, he was free to go to the nursing home, then spend the rest of the day preparing what he would write. He still didn't know how much he could or would tell about John.

Because of the final week schedule, nobody was following a usual routine. He had caught a glimpse of Becky going in for her math test early this morning, but he hadn't seen any of the rest of the gang at all. Finishing cleaning out his locker, he stuck the combination lock in his jeans pocket. It was like moving away, leaving him with a strange empty feeling — his "niche" at school, no longer his. Passing closed doors where students were bent over papers, writing furiously, he went outside; and as he cut through a worn place in the hedge that bordered the parking lot, he saw Bunnie.

"Bunnie!" he said, glancing around for signs of Jake or Clay, or any of his own friends.

"Hi." She was looking, too, but she was alone; there was no one else on the deserted school grounds.

"Do you have a final this afternoon?"

"Yes. French." Her voice was still whisper soft.

Mark looked at his watch. "You're way early. It's only eleven-fifteen."

"I know, but I wanted to study in the library for a while."

"Oh." Mark fingered some coins in his pocket. He'd been looking her over, he realized, for more cuts and bruises. He couldn't see any, but she seemed tired and her clothes were rumpled. "Ah, how are you doing?"

Bunnie shrugged. "Okay, I guess."

"I've — ah — been wondering about you. What happened with Jake?"

"Nothing!" Bunnie said. "But I hid all day Monday and yesterday, waiting for him to cool down. He was fine with me this morning."

"You *hid?*" Mark repeated her word. "Where?"

"At the airport," Bunnie said, matter-of-factly. "He'd have found me at home, and besides —" her voice dropped — "I already told you how it is there."

"You mean you stayed two whole days — and nights — at the airport?" Mark couldn't believe it.

Bunnie smiled sadly. "It's the safest place there is. You get hassled at the bus depot."

"Bunnie! Why didn't you tell me? You could have stayed at my house. My folks would have —"

"Oh, no, Mark." Her long blond locks swayed back and forth. "I've caused you enough problems already. I —- couldn't even let myself *think* about you since — then."

"Oh." It felt to Mark as if a piece had suddenly dropped into place in a puzzle. Since Sunday and the Arcade, he'd felt uncomfortable, as if something was missing. And that was it! He hadn't felt that invisible link with Bunnie — not once. Mark shook his head as if he could shake off the feeling that was rising in his throat.

"What's the matter, Mark?" Bunnie asked softly.

He blinked her into focus. "I'm just plain crazy," he said. "Do you know what I'm feeling now?"

"No. What?"

"Disappointment." The word exploded out of him. "I can't believe it. Disappointment. I've been angry. Upset. My whole life has been turned upside down and inside out because of your mind zaps. I've ignored them. I've willed them away. I've fought them. And now that they've stopped, I feel disappointed." He kicked at a rock on the ground — missed it.

Bunnie was watching him cautiously. "I just didn't think it was fair — or right — to keep leaning on you, Mark. I — It's not only that, either. You-you —" She looked down. Her hair covered her face, hiding her eyes. "I *had* to stop thinking about you. It would be too easy for me —" Her voice was fading away. "— to care too much for you."

Mark's stomach tightened. His breathing faltered. Guilt propelled, his thoughts boomeranged to Becky, like camera shots Before and After. Becky, laughing, having fun, Becky with her quick temper. After — Becky, subdued, cringing, hiding, looking as much victimized by him as Bunnie had by Jake. Spiraling still, the focus shifted back to Bunnie, and the unwanted thought pushed through. *And I wonder if I could care too much for you, too. In some ways we are already so in tune —*

Like the power of the unseen wind, cross currents of silence swirled between them.

Bunnie's hair fell away from her face, uncovering moist green eyes tinged with hope. She looked up at him, and Mark felt his world under attack — missiles of guilt and confusion, and an almost overpowering urge to hug her fears away, hold her, for whatever reason.

He clenched his fists, fighting himself, and half-turned, not to see her. "Bunnie, I don't know. I — just don't know." *If I'm going to lose Becky anyway —* the thought wouldn't form. "I need time." He spun around to leave, then stopped. The voice that came out of his mouth was a shock — forceful, demanding, possessive. "But don't be afraid to — to let me know if you need me. I *want* you to. Understand?"

He threw his stack of books onto the hood of his car, then dipped back through another cut in the hedge.

Emotions erupting through his feet, he began to run. He ran and ran, trying to escape the thoughts that wouldn't leave him alone, trying to outrun the fire that flamed at his temples. Now what had he done? Poor Bunnie. As if it hadn't been hard enough for her already — without encouraging her. Why hadn't he said, "Impossible!" or "But, you know, Becky and I —" or laughed or — almost anything besides what he had done, standing there with his mouth gaping open. He felt a wave of self-repulsion at his echoing words. "Bunnie, I don't know. I — need time."

But — The pavement clapped at his feet — *that response was real. No! It's Becky I care about — But Bunnie understands —*

He was out of breath, exhausted when his running finally brought him back to the car, sweaty and hot and emotion drained, in no shape to see John. His life was moving so fast that major events piled on top of each other with no time for integration. How could he cope now with one more thing? He scooped the scattered books off the car's hood and tossed them onto the back seat. On the other hand, he thought, maybe this is the best time to go. He had a feeling things weren't going to get any easier. And his exam was tomorrow.

Chapter Fifteen

A white curtain was pulled around John's bed and Mark hesitated, not knowing whether he should go in or not. "Hello," he said, "is anyone here with John?"

There was a scuffle of feet behind the curtain and a thin, raspy answer. "Yes, I am."

Mark wondered who was in there. "M-may I come in? I've come to see John."

"Well, I suppose so." But there was a warning in the tone.

Mark stepped around the curtain and faced the voice's owner, a frowning woman with a tight-lipped mouth and harsh curls in her graying hair.

"I'm Mark Miller," he said. Standing between him and the bed, she reminded him of an angry animal mother, protecting her offspring from prey. "I came to visit, ah, I mean, to see John day before yesterday, and —"

"Oh, yes." The woman drew even more tightly into herself. "The boy from the High School. They told me about you, and how you upset John. What are you doing here?" She glared at him. "What do you want anyway? Can't you see how he is?" She spit out the last sentence.

Mark stepped back, unprepared for this attack. He looked at John, lying flat on his back in the bed, his face reflecting nothing. "Hi, John," he said quietly. "Is this Mrs. Talbot?"

"He can't talk." She said each word separately.

"I know," Mark said; then attempting to smile he asked, "You are John's wife, aren't you?"

"Yes." Her answer was curt.

"You must have had an awfully hard three years since his stroke, haven't you?"

Her face relaxed a tiny bit as she nodded.

What could he say to put her at ease? He started talking, going with whatever came into his head. "When I decided to write a paper on the nursing home, I didn't know about John. I suppose it was just chance that the nurse brought me into this particular room, but she did. And ever since, I haven't stopped thinking about John. Last night, I even talked with someone else about him, to help me understand."

As he talked, it seemed that she gradually dropped some of her defenses. "Mrs. Talbot," he said slowly, "do you think John can think?" He went on before she had a chance to answer. "I kept wondering about that. Is his mind, his brain, working? Is he understanding us now?" He looked to her for a reply.

Mrs. Talbot sighed and sank down onto the edge of her chair, still holding her back stiff. "I believe so. It's more a feeling I have than anything else, but, yes, I do."

"I do, too," Mark said, his heart beating more quickly. "In fact, I *know* he does."

Color drained from Mrs. Talbot's face. She clutched the arms of the chair, making tendons and knuckles stand out white. "How? You can't know that. Not even the doctors know that."

"I'm sorry if I'm upsetting you. I know I'm only a kid, and I can imagine what you must think of me, coming in here like this. But — but — I'll try to explain. I — uh — I think I'm sort of a-a mind reader."

An exasperated gasp accompanied the sharp turn of Mrs. Talbot's head.

"I know it sounds crazy, but it *is* true. Sometimes I just know what's going on with other people. It's happened with a girl at school several times, and again, when I was here with John. We — we — communicated."

Mrs. Talbot's nostrils flared and her lips pursed even more tightly than before.

Mark leaned back against the window ledge. Her reaction was so like Becky's. "Look, Mrs. Talbot —" he was almost pleading — "if you would like to talk with John, I could help you."

Fright. Perhaps terror swept over her face, and disbelief. "I think you should get out of here, young man," she said. "I don't need anything more to torment me."

"All right," he sighed, "I'm sorry." Knowing he couldn't push her any more, he stood, looking once more at John. "Good-bye, John."

Weighted down by his double failure, Mark walked slowly away. It *had* been more than he could handle, just like he'd warned Dr. O'Reilly. But poor John. And poor Mrs. Talbot. Maybe he should come back again when she wasn't —

"Wait." Her quavery voice reached out after him.

Surprised, Mark turned. Mrs. Talbot was standing at the foot of the bed, her hand outstretched toward him. "If there's any chance —" she said. "It can't do any harm, can it?" Concern begged in her eyes.

"No," Mark said, shaking his head. "I don't think it can."

Reverently, Mrs. Talbot moved the covers away from John's pink foot. "John," she said, in another voice entirely from the one she'd used on him. It was soft, melodic, and loving. "I am going to ask you a quesiton. Are you ready?"

Nothing happened.

"Did you hear what this boy said, dear?"

Still nothing.

"John, do you want —" she looked at Mark. "What did you say your name is?"

"Mark."

"Mark, here, to help us — talk to each —"

Before she had finished the question, Mark detected a slight movement of John's toe, more like a twitch, he thought, but to Mrs. Talbot, it was obviously significant.

"Yes, Mark." Her voice was strong now. Assured. "We want to try." She squared her shoulders and waited.

Mark sighed. He'd been holding his breath. "What

happens," he said, "is that I pick up on John's thoughts or feelings. You can either ask him a question, or I can just listen for what he wants to tell you."

"I've been asking questions and more questions, but I never know if I'm asking the right ones. Let him tell me what he will."

"Okay —" Mark swallowed hard. What if it didn't work this time? What if he'd raised her hopes and couldn't do anything? He pulled away from the negative thoughts and concentrated on his breathing. In — slowly. Out — slowly. In — slowly. Out. Eyes closed, he eased into a no-space, no-thought, no-desire level of waiting.

He had drifted for what seemed a long time, nearing sleep, when the first image came through, one of concern and warmth and love, and the name, Alice. That part was clear, but then, fragments of thoughts and feelings, all jumbled together, bombarded him like garbage falling from a dump truck, impressions from a body unable to scratch an itch or blow its nose; of its pain, hurting bones, burning flesh. Useless, a prison.

"Stop!" Mark cried aloud and let go, escaping John's world. He opened his eyes and blinked. He was shivering. It was nearly dark outside. How long had it been? As he inhaled, shivers vibrated from his shoulders down his arms and into his finger tips. Feelings. His own feelings. "Oh, John," he sighed. "I don't know how you stand it."

"Mrs. Talbot," he said, "Alice? I couldn't finish. It-it was too hard. But —" He struggled to translate into words. "— the first thing he wants you to know is that he loves you."

It was as if he were standing on the edge of a bottomless pool of water, daring himself to dive, afraid that he would never surface again. Scared. More scared than he had ever been before. In the half-light, Dr. O'Reilly's words came back to him. "Remember. You are only a vehicle — a channel, like the bed of a river which allows the stream to flow through." And another memory overlapped the first, something about water — and hope. Even now, in this bizarre situation? He wondered. Maybe, he thought, especially now.

"All right, John," he said. "I think I'm ready."

But this time it was different. The connection, the impression was not of chaos, but rather of peace. He felt a glowing presence, an anticipation and longing toward beauty, comfort, harmony. And light. Everywhere there was a glowing whiteness. Mark was drawn, like a magnet, and lingered there.

Time, space, reality became one and nothing.

"Mark!" From somewhere far away a voice called to him. A hand out there shook his shoulder, but he resisted acknowledging that it was his shoulder, that he was being wrenched back into himself. Rising as if from a deep sleep, he opened his eyes. Mrs. Talbot was staring at him, her hand shaking him gently. "Are you all right?" she asked.

Mark nodded.

"You were so long. I was worried — Did you — Did John say anything?"

See — hear — say. Words were inadequate. How could the senses describe that which is beyond body? "I-I don't know," he said, slowly; then the understanding came home. He *did* know. John had shown him.

"Mrs. Talbot," Mark said, "you husband sees another place — another dimension of life beyond this. There, it is beautiful, peaceful. There is no pain. No body prison. He — he wants you to let him go there."

"Me?" Mrs. Talbot said, astonished. "How?"

Mark's hand slipped into his jeans' pocket and bumped into warm metal. Surprised, he drew out the forgotten padlock. He stared at the closed loop, then looked up at Mrs. Talbot. "Please, Mrs. Talbot, excuse me. I don't really understand what I'm about to say. But your love and concern may be locking John in, keeping him from moving on. You may be willing him not to die." Unconsciously his fingers turned the tiny dial. "He needs release." Softly he added, "Let him go." The lock in his hands sprang open.

Mrs. Talbot sat, clinging to her own hands, twisting a gold wedding band. It was completely dark outside now.

Only the light from the hall illuminated the room through the white curtain, shining silver on her rivulets of tears. Something inside her already knew, Mark realized. It had to. Otherwise, she would never have listened.

He was standing at the foot of the bed, not wanting to disturb her, when John's last message came.

Thank you, Mark. And good-bye.

Chapter Sixteen

In the cool evening robins chirped their final vespers, but Mark felt heavy, lifeless. It wasn't just that he would never see John again. Everything was coming to an end. Instead of celebrations, he was surrounded by deaths, large and small. He slumped down on the ledge by the sidewalk outside the nursing home and let the numbness seep over him. Like the blackness of night that was creeping across the valley, he was being engulfed in a blackness of the soul, a blackness he couldn't resist. Maybe *this*, he thought, is hell — losing everyone, losing even myself.

He turned to look at the nursing home. Were all those people in there lost to everyone, lost to themselves, too, like him? The window in John's room abruptly snapped into darkness.

Mark sighed. He slid off the ledge, scraping his back against its rough side until he was sitting on the ground.

Becky.

Even though he'd been with her every day this week — Monday at BoJo's, Tuesday here with John, last night at Dr. O'Reilly's lecture — it seemed as if he hadn't seen her at all — only her shadow, fading away from him. She hadn't been the same with him since that night in the car. "Oh, Beck!" he said aloud. Longing, guilt, rejection, confusion pressed down, suffocating him.

She didn't want to see him, she'd made that pretty clear. Or maybe she was as mixed up as he was, feeling tugs in a dozen different directions all at the same time. He did want to see her. He wanted to tell her what had just happened with John, to share things as they used to, but there was no way. She wouldn't listen.

In the valley the lights of the town began to flicker on. People were coming home from work, cooking dinner, watching the news on TV. Becky's house was there, too. And Becky.

Mark leaned his head against the hard cement. His gaze lifted above the town and lost its focus in the early twinkling stars. Time passed. His riling thoughts calmed.

He didn't know how long he had been there when suddenly he straightened upright and batted his eyes hard. Was it happening again? The spots? The zap? Or were the stars falling?

"Oh!" Mark sighed lightly, leaning back, grinning. "It's only you again! Back for the summer."

In the branches above him, in the bushes along the walk, fireflies beamed and ebbed, painting the night with their glowing. Mark chuckled as one landed on his knee, flashing its light on the rough texture of blue jeans. "Well, hello," he said, "welcome back." Another flitted around his tennie and landed on the plastic tip at the end of his shoe string, beeping its light. Others circled in their flight-paths closer and closer to him, as if they wanted their share of his attention, too.

Mark smiled, watching them sparkle with the lights from the town below and the stars above. "You're like them," he said softly, tucking his index finger under the one on his knee, "a little bit of heaven, and a little bit of earth." He drew the firefly close to his face. "Maybe there is light in my darkness after all."

"Mark!" Mrs. Hargrove said, opening the door. "How are you? We haven't seen you all week."

"It's been a pretty busy week," Mark said. "Is Becky home?"

"Yes, she is, I'll call her."

"Oh, Mrs. Hargrove," he said, "before you do, I'd like

to thank you — a little late — for the birthday party. It was really super."

Mrs. Hargrove smiled. "Well, we were glad to do it, Mark. You're welcome."

"And to apologize for —"

"Hey, Mark!" Tye barreled up the stairs from the den. "Look at what I made." He thrust a globbed-together bunch of papier mâché studded with flags and glitter and pieces of costume jewelry into Mark's face.

"All right!" Mark exclaimed, not wanting to admit he didn't know what it was. "That's terrific. Did you make it all by yourself?"

"Yep," Tye said proudly.

Mark looked back to Mrs. Hargrove, trying to finish what he'd started, but she smiled and patted his arm. "I'm sure you and Becky will work it out. Becky," she called upstairs. "Becky, Mark's here."

While he waited, only half listening to Tye's enthusiastic babbling, his stomach groaned at the lingering aroma of the Hargrove's dinner. He was famished. His mom would not be pleased that he'd completely forgotten dinner — again.

Becky appeared at the top of the stairs, but she didn't bound down as she usually did.

"Hi, Beck," Mark said, trying to disengage his hands from Tye.

"Hello, Mark."

There was an awkward silence. She reached the landing and stood a distance away from him.

"Ah, how was your math final?"

Becky shrugged. "Not too bad."

"I just have one more. Sosh tomorrow morning. Is that your last one, too?"

She nodded.

"What's 'sosh?' " Tye asked, tugging at Mark.

"Sociology," Mark said. "A class your sister and I have at school. Beck, would you like to go to the Dairy Queen? I forgot to eat dinner. I'm starved."

Becky glanced at Tye, then back at Mark. "Yes, I guess

we could," she said, "for a little while. Mom," she called, "is it okay if Tye goes with us to the D.Q.? We'll be back pretty soon."

"All right," Mrs. Hargrove called. "Wear your jacket, Tye."

Unfair. Mark wanted to protest, but it was too late. Tye was flying.

"Oh, boy! Can I get a D.Q. sandwich?"

"Sure," Mark said. Becky never used to play games like that, never used to want Tye around. What was she afraid of — him, or herself?

"Let's walk, shall we?" he suggested, hoping to snatch at least a few seconds alone with her, if they weren't imprisoned in the car with Tye.

It worked. "How fast can you run the rest of the way back to your house, Tye?" he asked later. "I'll time you. On your mark. Get set. Go!" He pressed his watch's stopwatch button. Tye's little legs swung to the sides as he dashed down the sidewalk.

"Becky," Mark turned to her, taking her hands. "I miss you. Where have you gone?"

"I'm right here," she said, holding her fortress.

"No, you're not. You're running even faster than Tye is," Mark said, then smoothed his voice. "Maybe that's what you have to do now, but I want you to know something — the way I feel about you hasn't changed one bit."

Becky hung her head.

"I'd like to take you to the Prom the happiest, most beautiful girl there — not like this. Not like you've been all week. I want my old Becky, full of fun and spirit." He paused, then added apologetically, "I know I haven't been quite normal lately, either, but I hope we can forget that for awhile and really enjoy the Prom."

"Mark," Tye yelled, "I'm home!"

Good!" Mark answered. Without looking, he stopped the watch. "Becky, I'm going on home now, but will you think about it? Let's enjoy these last few days of school and the Prom, and graduation, and then see what happens."

"M-a-a-a-rk," Tye yelled, "how fast was I?"

"Real fast, Tiger." Mark tilted the watch toward the streetlight. "Two minutes, forty-seven seconds." He turned to Becky again. "Okay, Beck?"

When she didn't answer, he said, "Well, good-night. Bye, Tiger."

"Good-night, Mark." She walked toward the house.

"Thanks for the D.Q. Sandwich," Tye yelled.

Mark opened his car door. "Oh, Beck." He suddenly remembered the corsage he hadn't ordered yet. "What color is your dress?"

"Blue," Becky answered. "Light blue."

Chapter Seventeen

Mark's heart leaped into his throat as Becky appeared at the top of the stairs, elegant in the flowing blue floor-length gown, her face radiant. Her lips parted in a little gasp when she saw him, and he smiled. He didn't look too shabby either, he knew, in the rented tux and ruffled blue shirt. Their eyes locked and all the accumulated tension Mark had felt about this night evaporated like a wisp of steam.

"But, M-o-o-m!" A wail floated from somewhere in the house, "I wanna see Mark 'n Becky!"

They both laughed. He stepped toward her and took her hand, feeling like a medieval knight, and led her toward him down the remaining stairs. "Oh, Becky," he said, aware of the awe in his voice, "you really are beautiful."

Becky blushed, and her smile deepened. "You are, too," she said.

And now his ears were warming. "Here. I-I brought you this." He handed her the white florist's box that he'd been cradling in his other hand like a football. He'd never realized how difficult it could be to choose flowers, but the more he'd looked, the less he liked first one and then another. For Becky it had to be special. Gardenias were too strong smelling. Roses seemed like a cliché. Finally, his choice had come from the north side of his own house — the tall, spring green stalks with strings of dainty white bell-like flowers that somehow reminded him of her — lilies of the valley. He'd taken them back to the florist to weave with baby's breath and foliage. He was sure no one else would have a corsage like that.

"Oh, Mark," Becky said, smiling up at him, "how

beautiful. And unique. I love it!" She smelled the delicate sweetness and lifted it for him to sniff. "And —" her voice dropped — "you were right. We *will* have a wonderful time tonight." She pulled the corsage pins from the green sticky tape on the back.

"May I help?" Mark offered, taking the pins. He stepped closer and gently — and a bit awkwardly — threaded the points through the translucent blue of her dress and the corsage. "There," he said, "I hope it stays on." He smiled down into her eyes. She was so close. He drew even closer and bent to kiss her lips. "Oh, Becky," he sighed. "Thank God. I thought I was losing you."

"Me, too," she said, swallowing noticeably, and then she laughed. It was the old spontaneous laugh he'd missed all week. "But we'd better go. Francine and Harley are waiting."

"Wow!" Harley exclaimed, walking with Francine in her peach-colored formal toward the car. "I'll bet it took you all morning to do that." Harley ran his fingertips over the high polish on the roof of the Fairlane.

"It did," Mark said, "all morning. Hands off !"

"Ohoo — Excuse me." Harley jerked his hand away then opened the back door for Francine. "Well," he said, admiring first Becky, then Francine, "I don't know who is the most beautiful —" he chuckled — "Mark or me!" Then he laughed again.

"Thanks a lot, Harley," Francine said, batting him with her clutch.

"You're sure in high spirits tonight," Mark said, and turned to look at Harley to be sure it was really he.

"You bet," Harley agreed. "This is *the* big night. Hey, Becky, why are you so quiet? You're not still moping, are you? Francine said —"

"Shut up, Harley!" Francine growled. "She's just nervous about playing at intermission, aren't you, Beck?"

Becky turned around, laughing. "No. I'm just fine. I'm not quiet and I'm not scared, either. I was just enjoying being Cinderella until you two clowns destroyed the atmosphere."

"Oohhhh," Francine said. "Why don't you make me feel like that, Harley, instead of talking about car polish?"

"Okay," Harley said. "I'll try." He snatched off his glasses and scooted across the seat toward her.

"Don't you dare wrinkle my dress!" Francine screeched.

"Jeez," Harley sighed and scooted back again. "Let's go, James. We're getting nowhere fast here."

Spring green and yellow crepe paper flowers and streamers and flickering hurricane lamps transformed the Rolling Oaks High School gym into a romantic wonderland, and as Mark led Becky in through an arched trellis, he was pleased that even the music was surprisingly good. Couples, all in formal attire, were already filling the dance floor, sparkling in the reflections from the revolving mirror-ball.

"It's hard to believe that we're the same clods who were grunging around in blue jeans and sweats taking finals yesterday," Mark said into Becky's ear.

"It sure is," she agreed. "Hi, Annie, Hi, Tom." She waved and they stepped out of rhythm to join the latecomers.

"Wow! Do you look nice or do you look nice?" Tom said, whistling. He looked at both Francine and Becky, but, Mark noticed with a surge of pride, mostly at Becky.

"You, too. Isn't this great?" Becky wriggled with pleasure, like a puppy. "They really did a nice job decorating."

More couples were floating in through the trellis behind them, and they moved deeper onto the dance floor. "Shall we?" Mark asked.

He could hardly believe it when the band stopped and the lead singer announced intermission. "Already?"

Becky's eyes stretched wide and she tried to see her watch. "I had no idea." she gasped. "Oh, I've been having so much fun. What a drag to have to play "Rondo Capriccioso" for the millionth time now. I'd rather stay with you and have some punch." She panted. "I'm so *thirsty*."

"Come on, Becky," Harley said, coming toward her through the crowd; "we're supposed to go up now. You're first."

"I'll get you some punch while you're playing," Mark said. "Play well. Let it flow."

The gym was beginning to smell once again more like a gym than a dance hall as hot, sweaty bodies surged *en masse* toward the refreshment tables, Mark among them. Over the roar of conversation he could barely hear the opening arpeggio of Becky's number. Nobody was really listening.

He got two cups of punch and was headed back to where he had been standing with Becky when he heard someone call his name and touch him lightly on the arm. He turned. "Bunnie!" he exclaimed. But then all he could do was stare. Her long locks were gone, her hair, cut into an attractive short style. Her skin seemed radiant and clean, and the gobs of black make-up around her eyes had been replaced with only a slight touch of color above her eye-lids, making her green eyes an even deeper green. Instead of a long elegant formal, she wore a simple stylish dress, a darker green than her eyes with white trim. Nice, but a strange choice for a Prom. "You — you look great!" Becky's piece rose to a crescendo in the background.

Not only Bunnie's appearance had changed. Mark sensed it was more than that when she looked him squarely in the eyes, no longer ducking to hide in a shield of hair. She smiled. "Mark, I want to thank you. I have to tell you before I go, so you will know how much you have helped me."

"Go?" Mark said, still holding the two cups of punch. "Where are you going?"

"I came tonight with Jake. I wanted to. He promised that he wouldn't drink, and I wanted to give him one more chance, but —" she sighed. "He and several others are already out in the parking lot, and they have a stash of pot and booze and sleeping bags and their old clothes —" She waved her hand, indicating more. "They are planning an all-nighter up in the hills. Jake doesn't know it, but I won't be there. Mark —" Her face lit up. "I'm leaving."

Mark had never heard her say so much at one time, or look so full of life and free of fear. She glanced at the doorway, checking, he supposed, for Jake's return, and he looked, too. He didn't see Jake, but Francine was right behind him facing the other way, but obviously listening to every bit of their conversation.

"I've got to go soon," Bunnie rushed on to say, "but Mark, I called my father this afternoon. I told him everything, about my mother — he didn't know — about the mess I've gotten myself into. And Mark, he wants me there with him. He made me reservations for tonight. Tonight! I'll be on the eleven-ten flight to Chicago before anyone even knows. Not my mother. Not Jake. Nobody but my dad and you."

"Eleven-ten!" Mark exclaimed, nearly spilling punch in his haste to see his wristwatch. He gulped down the drink, then holding the cup in his teeth, pushed his left sleeve with his right arm to see. "Bunnie, do you know what time it is? It's ten-twenty-two right now. How are you going to get there?"

"There's time," Bunnie said. "I'm going to call a cab now."

"But Bunnie. There's *not* time. You have to check in at least an hour before your flight. Don't you know that? And what if Jake catches you?"

Suddenly Bunnie's old expression of defeat and fear settled back over her face. Her shoulders slumped.

"Listen, Bunnie, don't give up. You're doing the right thing. But let me take you, okay? I have my car. I'll run you to the airport and then come right back. Francine —" He spun around, catching her off-guard. "Tell Becky. Explain what's happened, and tell her I'll be right back." He thrust the styrofoam cup of punch at Francine. "And give her this for me, okay?"

"Okay," Francine said, wide-eyed and red-faced. "Good luck, Bunnie."

"Thanks," Bunnie said.

"Let's go." Mark sprinted toward the door.

Chapter Eighteen

Mark and Bunnie ran from the school toward the short-cut in the hedge. Mark's brain was whirling, planning what he would do if they ran into Jake, calculating the fastest route to the airport, praying that Becky would understand. She *had* to. Francine heard it all. Becky would have done the same thing he did if she'd been in his shoes — anyone would have.

He cut through the hedge first, but stopped so quickly that Bunnie rammed into him from behind. Jake's group was huddled together, cigarettes glowing, between them and the car. Mark pivoted on one foot, and crouching below the level of the hedge, crept behind it to the next opening. There wasn't time for this. He squelched the urge to make a run for the car and take off. "Bunnie," he whispered, "let's try to get to the car without them seeing us."

She nodded, then followed him back along the parking lot side of the hedge, but the gravel underfoot refused to be silent.

"Hey," someone called out from the huddle, "who's that over there?"

Mark grabbed the keys with one hand and Bunnie with the other and shot out of the shadow toward the car, opening the door.

"It's Bunnie!" someone said, "with that guy, Mark."

"Hey, Jake," another voice challenged, "you gonna put up with that?"

Like a wild man, Jake burst from the group in a mad dash for Mark's car. He grabbed Bunnie's door.

"Wait, Mark," Bunnie said coolly as he started up the engine. She rolled down her window just enough to talk through it, and in a surprisingly calm voice said, "Jake, I'm leaving."

"You're *my* date! You came with —"

"Jake, just listen to me for once. I am leaving. For good. You won't see me again."

"What the hell are you talking about, you stupid bi —"

Bunnie raised her voice, interrupting his tirade. "I hope, Jake, for your own sake, that you'll come to your senses someday. You *could* be a pretty decent guy. Good bye, Jake." Then softly she said, "Okay, Mark, let's go, before he gets crazy."

Mark backed the car slowly to avoid hitting the onlookers.

"Hey! Hey!" Jake was yelling now. "You don't think I'm going to let you get away with this. Miller, you'll get yours. That's *my* girl!"

They weren't even out of the parking lot before Jake's car was roaring at them from behind.

"Oh, my God!" Bunnie exclaimed, flying forward in the seat as bumper jostled bumper. "He's insane. He'll do anything!"

Mark pulled into traffic and quickly cut in front of another car into the middle lane, protecting them on the side and back with a buffer of cars. He drove craftily, watching Jake's frenzied darts from lane to lane in the rear view mirror, timing green lights to be the last one through, all the way across town. As he pulled away from the last stop light before the two-lane highway that led to the airport, Jake was a block behind, waiting at another traffic signal. The Fairlane shot out into the dark countryside, Mark's foot pressing to the floor. "There," he said, exhaling the pent-up air in his lungs. "We've got a lead on them. What's the time?"

"Ten forty-seven," Bunnie answered, inhaling the numbers.

Mark concentrated on the road whizzing beneath them — he'd never driven so fast. "Bunnie," he said, "your luggage. Don't you have any?"

"It's at the airport, in a locker. I took it this afternoon."

"Did you check in, then, too?"

"I went to the airline counter, if that's what you mean. They gave me my tickets."

"Good," Mark sighed, easing up on the accelerator, but it was too late. Two lights, one red, one blue, began flashing behind him. "Oh, no!" he moaned, pulling over onto the shoulder. "We'll never make it now."

He opened his door and jumped out, meeting the police officer half way. "We're in a terrible hurry, sir," he said.

"I can see that," the patrolman replied, studying Mark's clothes that seemed to pulsate in the flashing lights.

"The girl in my car has an eleven-ten flight, but there's a carload of guys trying to keep her from going." He pointed. A car was just rounding the curve, going fast. "They've chased us clear from the High School. They've been drinking and —"

The officer pivoted as tires squealed and Jake's car pulled a U-turn right in the middle of the highway and veered, like a top about to tip over, back in the direction of Rolling Oaks.

"For the lova' — OK, kid. I believe you. Go on, but take it easy."

The officer ran to his car and spun around, siren blasting.

"I hope he gets them." Mark said, accelerating. "At least now they won't hassle you at the airport. "What time is it?"

Bunnie held her watch near the dash light. "Ten-fifty-five," she said. "We can still make it. Even on the bus, it only takes eight or ten minutes from here."

"Mark," Bunnie said hesitantly, "I really do appreciate this. You-you'll never know how much you've helped me. My father —" Her voice was almost reverent. "He really didn't know. He's a good man, a real gentleman. He's — he's a lot like you, Mark. No wonder he divorced my mother."

The airport tower was clearly in view now. Strings of runway lights dotted the ground. "But that's all over," she continued. "You made me see that nobody can force me to be anything I don't want to be. I'm starting over. A new life. A new me."

Tightness gripped at Mark's throat — pride, he guessed it was, pride in Bunnie, and in himself, too. He *had* helped. "Bunnie," he said, fishing for words, "you'll be fine now. Just forget the bad stuff that's happened."

"Oh, no," Bunnie said. "Never! I'll never forget. If I do, I might make the same mistakes again."

"Well —" Mark turned into the lane marked Departing Passengers Only. "I doubt that. But —" he smiled, glancing over at her, ungluing his eyes from the pavement for a second. "If you ever do need help, please — *don't zap me*. Chicago's too far away."

Bunnie laughed lightly. She was peering through the windshield as if she'd never seen the terminal before. "Funny," she said, "this place has been my escape so many times, but I never thought —"

Mark slammed on the brakes in the unloading zone. The clock above the door said 11:03.

"Mark, thank —"

"I'm going with you," he said, jumping out.

"This way." She pointed and they ran.

"Give me your locker key," Mark panted, "and I'll get your stuff. Go on to the desk. Stall them."

The boarding area was almost empty, but the loading door was still open and Mark could see the plane through the plate glass window. Bunnie was waiting for him. "We made it!" he puffed, handing her the suitcase.

"Thanks, Mark," she said, "for everything. I'll — never forget you." Then she rose up on tiptoes and kissed him, a soft, tender, good-bye.

Mark stood, rooted to the carpet and watched her disappear into the airplane. She didn't turn back, not once.

"Tough, isn't it, fella," an attendant said, startling Mark when he stepped in front of him to lock the door.

"Oh!" Mark's gaze zoomed up to the clock. It was 11:15. He had to make it back for the last dance with Becky. He just had to. Running as fast as he could in slick-soled dress shoes, he dodged through the late-night travelers back to his car.

Chapter Nineteen

When Mark pulled back into his parking place in the school lot it was 11:49. He'd made it in thirty-five minutes without breaking the speed limit, in time for the last dance. When he saw that Jake wasn't there waiting for him, he felt a pleasureable ripple of revenge, imagining that patrolman nabbing him. It served him right.

Quickly he ran a comb through his hair and hurried inside. The gym was packed, the lights now lower than ever and the band was playing an old slow number which had drawn the dancers into each other's arms. Mark scanned across the swaying people; then he stood on a folding chair by the wall for a better view. But it didn't help. Everything and everyone blended together in the star-spangled misty blue haze. He edged around the gym, straining to see Becky, dancing or sitting, but as he doubled around the far end without seeing her, he was hit with the sobering feeling that something was wrong. He hadn't seen Francine or Harley, either.

"Tom!" He darted onto the floor, grabbing Tom by the shoulder. "Have you seen Becky?"

Startled, Tom shook his head. "Not for a while. Did you lose her?" he joked.

Mark didn't answer. "Have you seen Harley and Francine?"

"Earlier," Annie said, "just after intermission. Hope you find them."

Mark rushed on, weaving through the crowd as the music lulled and the announcer crooned into the mike that this would be the last dance. The song — another slow dreamy one — lured everyone into a final romantic fantasy — everyone except him. His throat constricted almost to the point of strangulation, he jostled his way along the other side of the gym in front of the band, searching.

As he completed the circle back at the trellis, he stood paralyzed by indecision. Where could she have gone? Home? And where were Harley and Francine? Not thinking of anything better, he decided to check the rest rooms. He couldn't imagine that they'd be there, and they weren't. He ducked back into the gym.

"Mark!" Francine rushed up to him, "Oh, thank goodness you're back," she said in a hushed, urgent voice.

"What's wrong?" Mark asked. "Where's Becky?"

"Mark —" Francine's eyes were wide, apologetic. "I told her — everything — all about Bunnie and how she was leaving — and everything. And Mark, *I* think it was a real nice thing you did to —"

"Where is she?" he interrupted.

"She — she got real mad. She wasn't even thinking. She was just so mad that you'd gone off and left her again that she would have been mad no matter what the reason."

"Harley!" Mark wanted to strangle Francine and her endless beating-around-the-bush. "Where *is* she? Did she go home? What?"

Harley shook his head. "Jake came back in here —"

Jake! A wave of nausea swept over Mark as the word, then its impact, hit. "She didn't!" he gasped.

Harley nodded.

"We tried to talk her out of it, didn't we, Harley? But she was so crazy mad at you. Jake came sashaying up to her with some line about how you'd run off with his date — 'so you just come along with me, Becky, and we'll show them both.'" Francine mimicked Jake's come-on. "He was real smooth."

"She went with him, Mark." Harley bit his lip.

"She's in real trouble." Mark slumped down onto a folding chair. He remembered what Bunnie had told him about the woodsie, and Jake's promise of revenge. He knew from Bunnie that Jake could be devious. Becky, poor innocent, naive, hot-headed Becky, had become the pawn, Jake's way of getting back at him. "When?" Mark jumped up out of the chair. "How long ago?"

"Twenty, maybe twenty-five minutes."

"I've got to find her!" He ducked under the terrace, but Harley grabbed him.

"Where, Mark? How?"

"Bunnie told me they've got a woodsie all set up. He'll take her up there and —" He couldn't say the word.

"But where?"

"I don't know!" Mark wrenched away from Harley's grasp.

The music ended and dreamy couples began edging past them.

"Hey!" Mark called out to them, "Does anybody know where the woodsie is?"

People looked at him as if he were crazy.

Mark jostled into the gym, buffeting the crowd, accosting first one startled couple, then another. "Where's the woodsie?"

"You, Mark?" someone laughed. "You? Going on a woodsie? I can't believe it."

"Who with?" a caustic voice added, "Buxom Bunnie?"

"Doesn't anyone know?" Mark ran through the crowd, yelling now. "There's a woodsie somewhere up in the hills tonight. Where is it?"

A heavy hand on his shoulder abruptly stopped him. "What's going on, Mark?" He pivoted to find himself face to face with Mr. Jaramillo.

"Jake! Jake and that bunch — they're having a woodsie. I've got to find it," he panted. "Becky's with him."

"Becky?" A second shock wave swept over Mr. Jaramillo's face. His color was draining, leaving him ashen gray.

"I've got to go," Mark said, pulling away from him. He ran back across the dance floor. The lights were on now, and the band was packing up, the mystique gone.

"What are you going to do?" Harley said, intercepting him.

"Find her." Mark rushed ahead, trying to outpace his fear. Taking on the toughest gang in school, out in the hills — alone, outnumbered by who knows how many to one — It was insane. "I've got to!"

"We're coming with you," Francine panted, tottering behind in her high-heeled shoes.

The Fairlane spewed out of the parking lot, dusting formals and roses in its wake.

"Slow down, Mark." Francine begged as he tore into traffic. He cut back off the main street toward the dirt road that led up onto the mesa behind the high school. Fish-tailing on the gravel and washboard, he pushed to the top and jumped out. "Look for a fire," he said, scanning the hills surrounding the valley. His heart was pumping double time; he was as tense as an arrow ready to be shot.

"Good thinking, Mark," Harley said, patting him on the back, "but you've got to calm down. They could be anywhere. Let's think about this. They wouldn't have gone back where Pixie was k — where the accident was last year —"

Mark's teeth clenched. In his mind, he saw again Jake's veering car and the extent of Becky's danger. They could crash, go over — anything.

"Hey, look!" Francine pointed across the valley in the direction of the nursing home, but higher up, above the mesa behind it. "There. Do you see it? It's just a faint glow; it could be a campfire."

"Where?" Then Mark spotted it, too, a dim semi-circle of yellow-gold light. "There aren't any houses or anything up there."

"I don't think so," Harley agreed.

Mark was already back in the car.

"Good grief, Mark. Don't run over me." He hadn't noticed that Francine was only half in the car when he started backing.

He by-passed as much of the town as he could, then pushed the gas pedal to the floor as they hit the slope. The engine clanked, straining to gobble up the road, around curves and up onto the mesa.

"How will we ever find it?" Francine was leaning over the back of the front seat.

"It's got to be off this road somewhere. This is the only way up here. Just keep looking."

"Look back, too, Francine. You'll get a different angle," Harley said. "I'll watch the sides."

The mesa leveled out and Mark sped across it, quickly reaching the next rise. The car slowed and they started up again, swerving around more curves in a small winding valley.

"There! There it is!" Francine yelled, but they'd all seen it — the unmistakable glow of fire to the right and ahead. It slid out of sight as they navigated the next curve. Mark's hands held the steering wheel in a death grip. If Jake *had* done anything to Becky — if he's — but he didn't know what he'd do. He slowed down and reached for the light switch.

Francine gasped as the car was enveloped in darkness. Mark's night vision came quickly. There was a moon. It wasn't hard to see the small dirt road that led off toward the campfire. He'd drive in slowly, lights off, and if it came to it — "Harley," he said, "will you fight?"

Harley's "Yes," was strangled.

"Francine, you'd better wait in the car."

Mark's mind was functioning like a computer as he peered through the darkness. He turned off the pavement, and suddenly a fence loomed up before him. He stamped on the brake, sliding into barbed wire and a sign.

The realization came slowly. "Oh, no!" he groaned, reaching for the knob. The headlights flicked on to the sign, SANITARY LAND FILL.

"It's the dump! It's only the dump, caught on fire again."

Defeated and hopeless, he backed out and turned toward Rolling Oaks. Becky, he cried inside, where are you?

"Now what?" Harley finally broke the gloom.

"I don't know," Mark managed to answer.

They were crossing the mesa, nearing the edge where it dropped down into the valley toward town when the Fairlane missed the first time, slowed, caught again, sped up, then missed and coasted to a stop.

"We're out of gas," Mark said. It was one o'clock.

Chapter Twenty

"One - two - three - push!" Mark said, straining into the back of the car. Slowly it began to roll across the flat-topped mesa. "Come on, Harley. Push!"

"I *am* pushing," Harley grunted. "Mark — we've got to think —" he puffed, "of a plan — something — logical —"

The Fairlane reached the edge of the mesa and the impetus of their efforts carried it forward, gaining momentum. The car pulled away, leaving them staggering behind it.

"Francine! Put on the brakes!"

Red tail lights flared and Mark's giant strides catapulted him downhill and splayed him, hands out over the trunk of the car. He stumbled around to the side and jerked open the door. "Scoot over, Francine."

"No way!" Francine clutched the steering wheel. "The way you've been driving, you'll get us all killed. I'm driving."

"Francine," Mark started to argue, but they were losing time. "Oh, all right." He slammed her door, ran around the car, and jumped in. Panting, Harley slid into the back seat.

Francine released the brake and the car eased into a coast.

"I'm going to call Becky's parents." Mark said, "I think they should know what's going on."

"Oh, no," Francine moaned. "Poor Becky. Poor *you*, having to tell her folks."

They were moving faster now, plummeting down into the valley.

"We can get gas at that station at the foot of the hill," Harley said. "I'll pump while you call."

Mark felt as if there was an inflated balloon in his throat as he dialed Becky's number. The phone rang three times before anyone answered.

"Hello?" It was Becky's dad.

"Mr. Hargrove," Mark said, "this is Mark. I, uh, thought you should know what's happening."

"Yes, Mark?" His voice was kind, patient, as if he expected Mark to ask if Becky could stay out another hour.

"A friend of mine needed some help at the Prom and I left for about an hour to take her to the airport. It all happened so fast, while Becky was playing her piece, that I couldn't —" He blurted out the whole story. "— but this Jake is a mean character, Mr. Hargrove. I'm worried. He's out to get back at me, through Becky."

"Mark," Mr. Hargrove interrupted, "I want you to call the police. Right now. Then I'll call them and back you up."

Mark choked. Call the police! "A-all right, Mr. Hargrove." In the background he could hear Mrs. Hargrove asking, "What happened? Is Becky all right?"

"And, Mark," Mr. Hargrove added, "you did the right thing, telling us. Thanks. Now call the police." The line went dead.

Shakily, Mark dialed 911. It was an emergency, after all. A woman's tinny voice answered.

"I want to report a —" If he said woodsie, would she take him seriously? "— an abduction, a-a kidnapping."

"Yes, sir." *Beep* A sharp tone sizzled in his ear. "Your name, please,"

"Mark Miller. My girlfriend, Becky Hargrove —"

"What is your address, please?"

"114 Lincoln Way, Rolling Oaks, but —"

Beep.

"Telephone number?"

"994-3 —"

Beep.

"Please go ahead, sir. You are being recorded."

"— 275. Look!" he said, nearly exploding. "Time is running out! Can't I tell you what happened?"

"Yes, sir. The victim's name is Becky Hargrove?" *Beep.* H-a-r-g-r-o-v-e?"

"Yes." he snapped. Victim. His hands were shaking.

"What is her address?"

Mark felt that someone had stuck the filling station's air hose down his throat and turned it on. The pressure inside threatened to blow him up, like an old innertube. But when he finally got through their routine questions, he found that the police had already received a call from Mr. Jaramillo, and two cars had been dispatched.

"Only two?" Mark's voice spiraled away from him. He looked down at his watch. It was 1:30. "Okay, okay. Where have they looked?"

"One moment, please."

Harley had pumped gas, paid the cashier, and was waiting in the car. Mark had taken the extra few seconds to report the fire at the land fill before he finally hung up. "Okay." He jumped in the front seat. "Let's go. Head north, Francine. The police have two cars out looking, one between here and Cedar Run and the other along Highway 112. That leaves the Ferry Lake Road, Hanging Man's Gulch, the Coal Road, that road that goes up to the National Forest campground —" Mark followed his mental map, like a radar scanner, in a 360 degree sweep of the area. "— and —"

"And," Francine interrupted, "the Deer Creek Canyon Road and the road up to the old ski area, and all those little back roads that criss-cross everywhere, and places where there aren't any roads at all. Mark," she stated flatly, "we'll never find Becky this way."

Thud! Mark felt a jolt in his chest — a fleeting thought about heart attack — death. Francine was right. If Becky was — hurt, he'd rather be dead. And the longer she was out there with that — that animal, the worse her chances were. Bunnie's bruised cheekbone, her terror-filled eyes flashed before him. He slumped in the seat. "We've got to do something," he said, without the conviction of an idea.

Thinning city lights flicked past his window as Francine steered the Fairlane into the hills, turning onto a gravel road.

"Well, there may still be a way — " Harley said slowly, "if that E.S.P. of yours is worth anything."

"That's what's gotten me — Becky — all of us into this mess!" Mark exploded. "I've had it with E.S.P.! Becky was right! If I'd listened to her — "

"Maybe so!" Francine interrupted, impatience edging her voice, "but, like it or not, you'd better try! It's the only chance we've got. And it's not getting any earlier!"
"What ti — "

"It's nearly two o'clock," she snapped back, "and as trivial as it may seem, my parents are going to be worried about *me*, too."   Mark cringed. "Okay," he muttered. "I'll try it.'

He squared himself in his seat, tried to' remember how to do it. The tires jostling beneath him weren't as agitated as he was. Calm down, he lectured himself. That had always been a factor — relaxing.

He closed his eyes and tried to breath regularly, slowly, rhythmically, but the air hitched and wavered and that blown-up feeling in his chest wouldn't go away. Neither would the thoughts. And guilt. If he'd never left Becky in the first place, this wouldn't have happened. Bunnie could have taken a flight the next day or found someone else to drive her or — but he didn't buy it. It had been the right thing to do, regardless. And Becky should have understood. Slowly, he acknowledged his gradually-building anger. Becky's the one who should have known better. She got herself into this mess. It was her own fault.

But then he felt guilty at not feeling guilty, for blaming Becky instead of himself. His anger, really, was at himself, not her, at his inability to know what was right. Breaking promise after promise to Becky — that wasn't right. Leaving her alone at the Prom on "the best night of her life" wasn't right. But helping Bunnie hadn't seemed wrong — Frustrated, he blew out cheekfuls of air and opened his eyes.

"It's no good," he said. "Stop the car."

Chapter Twenty-One

Mark picked his way up the side of a hill and sank down onto a rock, pressing his head between his palms. To do nothing now was harder than fighting Jake or tearing up every mountain in sight, but he had to do it. It *was* his only chance. Maybe Becky's only hope. Do *nothing*. Not even think. Not imagine what might be happening to her.

Probably now nothing will happen, no thought, anger at "it" welling up inside. It comes when I don't want it to, doesn't come when I do. But gradually the warring thoughts diminished and he focused on her name. It was as if his mind, like a huge eagle, was soaring across the moon-light-silhouetted blue mesas and slanted hills, trying to pick up her sign.

But nothing. Nothing came. No sense of connecting with anything at all. No link. No impulse. No image. No voice. Only small night sounds and the soft rustled of wind through the oak branches.

Time, the silent enemy, advanced. Unable to bear its onslaught, he opened his eyes and sought the luminous face of his watch. It was 2:22. The numbers slapped at him, reminders of 3:33 and two other nights. But then from the corner of his eye, he saw another luminescence, like the hands of his watch. He turned. One lone firefly alighted on the stone beside him, blinking. On. Off. On. Off. On. Off. Mesmerized by the rhythm, Mark stared. On. Off. On. Off. On. Off. On. Off. And as he watched the flashing glow, his thoughts slowly began to fall away. Gradually, gradually, that familiar right feeling — as if he were suspended in some in-between place — started to return, and in its wake, a ripple of hope.

I'm getting it! But with that intrusive thought, it dissipated. He waited once again for his mind to clear of hope and disappointment, fixing his gaze on his pulsing guide. "Take me there again," he whispered.

Finally, faint images began to drift by. A bottle — a hand — a dirty green army blanket — flames. Like fleeting clouds building toward a storm, the images bunched together. *Where, Becky? Where?*

He quieted himself again. Breathe in. Out. In. Out. In. Out. In.

He could not have called it a vision. It wasn't as if he heard a voice. It was only an idea, but an extraordinarily powerful idea that seemed to come from beyond himself, and within it he "saw" a place — the jeep road up to the old abandoned gold mine.

Was that it? Was that where Becky was? The old mine?

His eyes opened wide in shock. The old mine? Mark's head jerked to the side as if he expected the firefly's confirmation, but the rock was dark. He looked to the right, to the left, up, behind him, but there was no sign of it, no light signaling in the darkness. Had it been there? Or had he only imagined it?

Tripping and sliding, Mark rushed down the incline toward the car. The mine was the last place anyone would look. The road up there was so bad that not even many jeeps used it anymore. In places it clung to the side of the mountain on a ledge of shifting slate.

"The old mine. Let's go!"

Francine stared. "You really — did it?"

"I didn't do anything. Come on. Let's go!" Mark panted. "I just got this impression of a fire and the old mine road."

"Are you sure?" Harley hunkered up over the front seat.

Mark shook his head. "But it's all we've got."

"Oh, poor, poor, Becky," Francine said, taking a curve too fast, braking too much.

The car slid sideways on the washboard surface and Harley tumbled. Hoisting himself back onto the seat he growled, "Slow down! You're as bad as Mark." Then, controlling the anger in his voice, he said, "If those idiots have driven up that gold camp road, and if we're going to follow them, we have got to be more than careful. It won't do Becky or anyone else any good if we go over the edge."

"I'm sorry," Francine said. It was the first time Mark had seen Harley overpower Francine. She shifted into second.

The gold camp road wound up, lazily at first. Mark leaned forward, scanning the ground in front of the headlights. Suddenly, hope spurted through him. "Look," he said, "fresh tire tracks in the dust."

"Oh!" Francine gulped. "I just hope they haven't gone too far." The dust-covered ruts were getting deeper and rougher. "Should I cut the lights?"

"No!" Harley exclaimed. "It's too dangerous. We could high-center. Besides, even if they do see us coming, they'll probably think we're some of them. Who else knows where they are?"

"Yeah," Francine agreed in a shaky voice, made even shakier by the road, "you're probably right. Boy! Am I ever nervous. What are we going to do when we find them? Oh, poor Becky!"

That was the same question Mark had been asking himself.

The road zig-zagged abruptly around a huge outcropping of rocks, and suddenly reflections from tail lights blinked out of the darkness ahead. "There they are," Mark whispered at the same moment Francine hit the headlights. The Fairlane bounced to a stop.

"Let's leave the car here," Harley said softly. "Maybe they haven't seen us yet."

"Okay," Then Mark changed his mind. "No. Francine, after you think we've gotten up to where they are, drive up there and turn around. Leave the lights off."

"But how will I know —"

"Wing it!" Mark snapped. He stepped out of the car and

stealthily pushed the door closed. Harley, behind him, did the same. Francine's plaintive whisper reached out the window after them, "Oh, you guys, be careful. Poor Becky!" In the moonlight they followed the rutted road to the parking area, and Mark recognized Jake's car immediately. He looked inside and saw empty beer cans crushed and twisted, gleaming in the moon's glow alongside Jake's discarded tux, and something white — Becky's lilies of the valley. He shuddered. Suddenly her danger seemed even more real — Jake pawing at her, Becky fighting back, losing her corsage in the struggle.

He rushed ahead. "Hurry up," he whispered. Not far away in the opening of a draw was the glow of a fire. Mark dashed toward it, stepping high, heedless of the dark.

"Ough!" Mark's foot stubbed against something soft and he pitched forward, nearly toppling, head first, into the ground. But he caught his balance and turned back. In the light from the fire, behind him now, he saw a sleeping bag and the white shoulders of its two occupants. "Sorry," he said, reflex habit. Then looking over the area he saw more — bottles, cans, clothes, and couples. His stomach turned.

"Becky!" he called out, shattering the silence. "Becky! Where are you?" He listened, then heard her muffled reply.

"Over here, Mark. Here."

His heart was pounding; anger coursed through his body making him ready. He ran toward her voice, scattering clanking bottles and cans everywhere. "Beck!"

She was on the ground with Jake in the dim shadows of the campfire. "You found me!"

He reached down and scooped her to her feet and holding her, backed away, watching an infuriated Jake, like an angered hibernating bear, lumber to his feet and stagger toward them, fists clenched. Through the soft folds of her once beautiful dress, he could feel Becky trembling, but he thrust her away from him into Harley's arms, never taking his eyes off Jake. "If you've done anything to her —" he said, feeling the primordial rage of an animal, "I'll —"

"I'm okay, Mark," Becky squeaked. "He didn't —"

But Jake lunged forward, fists up, eyes wildly reflecting the fire. His fist shot out away from his body. Mark ducked, but the impetus of the misguided swing carried Jake around in a dizzying circle and he landed in a heap on the ground, groaned once, and was out cold.

Mark stared. Jake was dead drunk. It was all over. Nobody was going to bother them now. He turned to Becky and took her gently into his arms. "Oh, Becky, Becky, Becky," he said, nuzzling her hair. Emotions collecting at the back of his throat threatened to choke him. "My poor Becky."

She clung to him, sobbing. "I'm s-sorry, Mark. I'm so, so sorry."

"Shhh!" he whispered. "You're okay now." Holding her by the shoulders, he pulled away. Her dress was torn at the shoulder and her face was smudged. He removed his tux coat and slipped it around her. "Are you — all right, really?"

She nodded. "He tried to —" Her breath jerked. "But he didn't —"

Mark looked back at Jake's twisted heap on the ground. His rage modulated into disgust. For some reason he didn't understand, he walked around Jake, plucked up the grungy green army blanket and dropped it over him. "Let's get out of here," he said.

In the back seat of the car, Mark held Becky close, listening to her breathing gradually change from hiccoughing gulps to a calmer rhythm. First her shivering, then the tension in her back lessened, but he could still feel one fist tightly clenched against him. "He-he tried —" She shuddered. "He pawed at me, like some sort of —" She shook her head. "And then he tried to - to smooth-talk me and get me mad at you again." Her breath hitched. "He tried to get me drunk —" A hint of laughter bounced in her voice. "But I outsmarted him. He kept giving me more and more beer, and everytime he did, he drank one, too, only I was sipping an empty can and dumping the other." She sniffed, giggles and tears all mixed together. "There's a beer lake up there now."

"He fell asleep with his arm over me. Yuck! I was afraid to move, so I just stayed there — I don't know how long — thinking about you, Mark." She pushed herself away from him and looked up into his face. "How did you find me? Did Bunnie tell you?"

"Well —" Mark hedged.

Francine glanced over her shoulder. "Tell her, Mark," she butted in.

"Yes, Mark," Harley agreed. "She ought to know."

"It wasn't Bunnie. I-I just got this image of the old gold camp road and a fire and —"

"I *knew* it!" Becky socked her still-clenched fist into her other hand. "I kept thinking about what you did with John, and I did it, too. I thought real hard about this place, over and over again, and somehow, I just knew you'd find me. But —" she said, holding out her fist, gradually loosening her fingers. "I wasn't totally unprepared in case you didn't." There in her palm lay the two long pointed corsage pins. "And I'd have used them, too!" The vicious tone in her voice softened. "But, you know," she said, "when Jake got real drunk, before he zonked out, he started to cry — over Bunnie. I felt kind of sorry for him, in spite of everything."

"Yes," Mark agreed, "I think I know what you mean." He slipped his arms around her again. He was warm and glowing all over. She'd signaled to him. She "knew" he'd find her. That could only mean that — that his being the way he was was okay with her now. "So you don't just think I'm a self-induced crazy anymore?" he asked, only half-teasing.

Becky's dirty face broke into a wide grin. "But of course I do, silly. You *are* a weirdo freak mind reader — thank goodness!" She smiled up at him with such a warm, loving, accepting look that Mark's heart threatened to stop altogether. "And I think," she said, eyes sparkling, "I think you're thinking what I'm thinking."

"What's that?" Mark asked, warily.

"That Harley and Francine should turn around."

And with that invitation, Mark pulled her to him. Closing his eyes, he felt her kiss respond, freely, without the faintest hint of doubt or rejection.

Breathless, she pulled away, but only long enough to whisper, "I love you, Mark."

"And I," he said, "love you."

And as they kissed again, the darkness outside exploded with the blinking of dozens and dozens of glowing fireflies.